A WITCH'S DOZEN

A WITCH'S DOZEN

JANET FOX

ILLUSTRATED BY

STEPHEN FABIAN

WILDSIDE PRESS
& W. PAUL GANLEY: PUBLISHER

Published by:
Wildside Press, P.O. Box 301, Holicong, PA 18928
& W. Paul Ganley: Publisher, P.O. Box
149, Amherst Branch, Buffalo, NY 14226.
www.wildsidepress.com
http://hometown.aol.com/weirdbook/myhomepage/index.html

Contents

Witches

He sat at the plastic counter and when his food, came everything was in little plastic packets. A look out of the huge plate-glass window showed him the road he'd been driving all day, a featureless ribbon of blacktop rolled out indifferently through gutted hills showing strata of yellow rock. He opened a packet and put the white powder into his coffee, stirring it with a white plastic spoon. He watched the liquid swirl muddily, undissolved granules of imitation cream bobbing on the surface. It occurred to him that he was as close to being nowhere as you could get. He left the turnpike just outside of Commercia, and the trees growing along both sides of the narrower highway engulfed the car in dancing patches of green-gold shadow, even more pronounced now that it was beginning to get dark. In the deceptive clarity of just dusk he saw something along the highway, a figure, slight, in jeans and a t-shirt, the shape seemingly distorted until one saw the canvas backpack. One thin arm was raised, the thumb extended. The same instinct which made him reject the plastic packets, put his foot on the brakes, tires gritting on gravel along the road's edge as he stopped. The figure, with an aptly feral movement, loped the few yards to the car, grasped the door handle. The light inside the car slid off very straight hair a color somewhere between red and gold. There were pale sun-freckles across the nose and cheeks and a mouth that seemed flexible to many expressions and now wore a furtive smile. The door slammed with an oddly inevitable sound.

"I'm going as far as Medicine Oaks, " he said, hearing the grouchiness in his own voice with a kind of surprise.

"Thanks, Mister."

He drove on, the car's interior now a capsule of darkness and silence except for the dim green glow of the dashlights. He'd seen the bud-tips of breasts under the thin cotton of the t-shirt and was filled with a vague unease. Only the nowhere feeling he was trying to outdistance had made him stop at night for a hitchhiker, a risky idea at best. She had put aside the backpack and was sprawled on the seat in apparent comfort. He'd been on the edge of delivering a lecture on the evils of hitchhiking for young girls until he realized he'd compounded the error by picking her up. It wasn't that she was in any danger from him.

He'd taught school, had children of his own, almost resented her posture of total relaxation.

"Are you going far?"

"I'm just seeing the country," she said in a rather sleepy voice.

"There isn't much country for tourists," he said, hoping to insinuate that he suspected she had run away from some nearby home.

"It's interesting," she said. "Nobody bothers you." Just as well she didn't seem to take his meaning, he reflected, since he might have to turn her over to the authorities at Medicine Oaks.

"Get many rides?"

"I didn't need one till now. I was traveling with someone."

"What happened? Or is it personal?"

"I don't know exactly. He was nice. He bought me these." She indicated the clothes and the knapsack. "But this morning I woke up in the hotel room alone; the motorcycle gone—Frankie too."

He was silent, with a last-of-the-dinosaurs feeling, wondering why it always surprised him, these girls putting on a casual sexuality with their training bras. But when he thought about it, he'd been left stranded, himself. Not that Cindy had run out on him; she'd done everything by the numbers. That was like her, managing the divorce like an elaborate dinner party—not to create publicity; that would be bad for her business, not to injure the children (they were like potted plants she moved so-delicately to avoid 'bruising the roots). "They're young," she said. "They'll adjust." He'd been awed by all of it, so that when the final papers came, he'd wanted to shake her hand, say "well done," but he'd left instead. He wondered why with all her careful building, he'd been able to see nothing but wreckage.

His headlights caught the doublestars of animal's eyes along the road, a blur of something small crouched in the border of weeds. Then, it was gone.

"What was that?" asked his hitchhiker, her voice a harsh whisper.

"Nothing. An animal along the road—a cat, maybe."

"I don't like cats." Her voice had an odd intensity. "Their eyes—they watch."

The lights of Medicine Oaks appeared, a starswarm on the side of the dark hills. It wasn't long before he was rounding the last wide turn and entering the main street, old fashioned buildings the color of dust lining it, overlaid with signs in garish neon. He knew where he was going to spend the night—a small dilapidated motel tucked away on a quiet side street. When he stopped in front of it, he debated for a moment. He didn't exactly want to drop her off at the police station in the dead of night and it wasn't safe to leave her asleep in the car.

He got a double, not quite wanting to pay for two cabins. When he tried to waken her she rolled away from him so that he had to lift her, sleeping exhaustedly, and carry her inside. He'd been a little worried about the arrangements at first, but it was only like carrying a sleeping child to bed. Her face was curiously lax and empty of expression, as if the body were untenanted, the mind wandering some dreamscape.

When she showed no sign of wakening, he paused a moment, then undid the button and fly of her tight-fitting jeans, pulling them off the slim childish hips in cotton panties, then drawing the blankets quickly up to her chin. He prepared himself for sleep, liking the incongruity of having her there in the other bed. Her breathing was the last sound he heard before he fell asleep.

And then he was wandering in his own dream country. The winds made a terrible racket moaning and whining , around the angular contours of a strange distorted house. An immense oak tree grew by the door, its bulk seared white on one side by some long ago lightning bolt, and blood-red creepers grew rank along one wall of the structure, fluttering in the constant wind. As he watched, the door opened and three beings came out to stand in the shelter of the tree, their patched and ragged garments tossed in the wind. Their faces were dark and indistinct but he got the impression of age and a grotesqueness that surpassed human ugliness. They seemed to argue over something, skinny arms gesticulating. "You've stolen it, you hussy, and you will be made to give it back!" He was awakened by a half-suppressed shriek and it was a moment before he remembered he wasn't alone in the room. The hitchhiker was sitting up, a hand over her mouth, the other held out as if to ward off some evil, her eyes large and dark with terror. He sat on the bed and put his arm around her. "Just dreams, honey," he said, as her half-shrieks subsided into sobs.

"They were going to bring me back there," she whispered, moving close to him. For a confused moment he thought she meant back to the strange house in his own dream. He became aware of her warm skin beneath the thin cotton shirt, the roundness of a breast against his wrist. It was one thing to tuck an inert sleeping body into bed—this was something else.

"I like it here," she said, looking up through the brassy-gold fringe of her bangs. "I like being close to you." He moved away abruptly. "There now," he said, feeling stupid as he retreated from her warmth. He was possibly old enough to be her father, but he wasn't all that old. Christ, but he'd been a fool to even consider this arrangement. He felt vaguely as if he'd been caught molesting a student, but nothing for it but to grit his teeth till morning.

Then he could leave her here without worrying about the authorities. He wondered wryly if the motorcyclist had been such a moral sort as himself. She only wept a little longer, the sound deadened by the pillow.

He awoke and was confronted by the prosaic seediness of the motel decor. That weird place and those figures—only a dream, and dreams, for all their clarity, were nothing at all in the morning. In the next bed his hitchhiker was opening her gamine's eyes. Only a child and even if she were the teenaged queen of tramps, she had nothing to fear from him. He'd never been interested in jail-bait, after all. As a teacher and as a father, he should have learned something about children.

"How about some breakfast?"

"God, yes. How did you know I was starving?" she said, bounding barelegged from bed.

"Just a lucky guess. I'm Michael Payton. What's your name ?"

"Rue."

"Ruth?"

"No. Rue."

He waited for a moment for a last name, but there was none coming. "You can get cleaned up and dressed in the bathroom. I'll buy you some breakfast, and maybe—well, let's just let the future take care of itself." He turned away and heard footsteps and then the sound of the shower.

Over breakfast in the cafe quaintly named "Mom's" he assumed his best teacherly manner, feeling now that he was in charge of the situation. "You won't prove anything by running away. Were they really so bad, your parents?"

She looked up stolidly. "I don't have any parents."

"Oh, I'm sorry. Well, who do you live with?"

"My sisters, but I can't go back there." She seemed to shudder a little.

"Were you mistreated? If you were, you wouldn't have to go home; there're places where you could finish school—"

"I do have a lot to learn about the world," she said with a mischievous smile.

"Sure, what if we went to the police station here, and—"

Her eyes wildly dilated and for a moment he thought she'd bolt from the booth, but she just crouched down against the window, making herself as small and unnoticeable as possible.

Outside on the raindamp pavement, two old ladies were watching them. One of them wore a bright flower-print dress on her sunken contours. They passed on by, their faces hidden by the umbrella.

By degrees Rue came out of her fearful, crouching stance.

"Did you know them?"

"Maybe—I'm not sure, but I've got to get out of here. You've got to take me with you—out of this town."

"You *are* on the run." He grasped her wrist, but a woman at the next table gave a shocked look and he let go. "You know I'll have to take you to the authorities."

Her mouth twisted into a smile, though her eyes had lost none of their terror. "Shall we inform them where I was last night?" she asked, her tone all innocence.

It was a moment before the anger came, before he realized just how neatly she had trapped him.

It was hot, the sun quickly drying the rain and creating a steam-bath atmosphere. Rue sat quietly, every so often turning to look out the back window as if she thought someone might be following. If she thought he'd forget the humiliation of this morning—

As he drove his anger cooled a little. He remembered her fear of those harmless old ladies, and how she'd cried out at night. He'd been thinking of stranding her along the road, but what if someone really dangerous picked her up? What she needed was help, maybe even the help of a psychologist. He resolved to keep her with him till he reached Salt City. Maybe he could reason with her, find someone to give her the help she needed.

The day was drawing to its sweltering close but he had every intention of reaching his destination before he slept, even though it would probably take half the night. The road here overlooked a large state lake. Wind chopped the waves a little, and there was a cooling breeze through the car windows. "Can't we stop here, just for awhile?" she asked. He'd been thinking of the same thing.

Grunting an ungracious assent he took the side road that would lead them down to the beach. As he turned off the motor, the noise of crickets scratched uneasy patterns on the silence. From here the highway was hidden and the narrow strip of sand beach was bordered with weeds.

Rue opened the door and slipped from the seat just as he told her to stop. She ran through the thigh-tall weeds until she reached the beach. Grudgingly he followed. The sun was clear amethyst seeping into a heat-blanched sky, the wind brushing at the gritty feel of his skin. When he thought again of Rue, he saw her jeans and t-shirt lying empty on the damp sand. She was just shedding her panties and he saw her narrow buttocks just before she splashed into the dark water. He sat down in a dry place, loosening the collar of his shirt and laying aside his glasses. He sat with his head in his hands for some moments wondering if his concern for this stranger was because he wanted to ignore his own problems. Then he asked himself "what problems," because it followed if you had no life, you had no problems.

When he looked up, the shadow-webbed water was unbroken; no head bobbed there. With an awful feeling of loss he ran along the edge of the water. He saw nothing at first, then something that could be a body floating. He shucked his trousers, shrugged out of his shirt, and splashed toward the dark floating something, ripples casting back a thousand shards of broken moonlight. She was face down in the water, turning lazily. He struggled to turn her over, his feet seeking uncertain purchase in the mucky bottom. He thrashed in the water, pulling her toward shore. Her skin was waxy-white in the dim moonlight, her limbs lax, her face totally devoid of expression. Frightened he hugged her close for a moment and when he could detect no breathing, he opened her mouth and with a forefinger checked for obstructions. He put his mouth on hers, breathed gently in.

Her lips moved; one small hand clutched the back of his neck and her tongue darted delicately between his lips, so startlingly that he didn't move away. He felt her other hand, small and cold, move down his stomach, insinuating itself under the waistband of his sodden briefs. It was as if the world as he knew it had come apart. Cricket noise subsided into a burst of deafening silence. In his arms he held the delicate, almost sexless body of a doll . . . or a child, but when he looked into the face, something incredibly ancient and wise looked out at him, certain of a response. With all this, there was still an element of surprise in it when his hands, gritty with sand, found her breasts.

When he came back to reality, the droning insect song, the clammy gray sand, still holding the random sketchmarks their bodies had made, the brittle weed bending in the wind, he saw Rue sitting beside him, her face showing a drowsy satiety, her hands moving over the contours of her own body. "You won't have it back," she said, but not to him—to the darkness beyond the crazily waving shadows of dry weeds, as if someone were standing there listening. But no one was. "It's mine now. To use as I will. To enjoy as I wish."

When he looked at her, she fell silent, reached for the t-shirt, though the dampness made it translucent. He was half afraid to touch her, but he moved closer, staring into her face with a kind of horror. "Who are you?" he asked, not admitting that the question might as well have begun with a what.

"What do you think I am? Do you think I'm a witch? Maybe I am." She hugged herself. "I like this place. I do. And I like you and Frankie . . . and the others, so very many new others. So many, many new things to try." She rose and danced a little along the deserted beach, a moving white shape among the capering shadows that paced her.

He slept in the car, waking with damp and wrinkled clothing a crick in his neck, and an indelibly soiled conscience. He'd half hoped Rue had gone off somewhere on her own, but she came climbing up the bank to the car, smoothing down her coppery hair, if he hadn't known better, the child he'd accompanied down to the water the night before, except he knew better. She'd stopped to up-end her sneakers, tapping the sand out of them. "It's not the end of the world, you know," she said as if sensing his mood.

"I just never quite thought of myself as a child molester," he said.

"Some things are real," she said, "and some things are only masks, hiding those things we don't know how to look at."

He didn't try to figure that one out; he just drove. There were only ten more miles to his destination when he felt too tired to go on. Leaving the highway for a small sleepy-looking town, he found a motel on the edge of it and pulled in.

"I'm dirty and tired," he said angrily.

Wind kicked up dust from the bare ground around the cabins. A lean and battered-looking orange tom-cat slunk from behind an untrimmed shrub and watched them for a moment with yellow-glass eyes, then withdrew. "I don't like this place. I think he recognized me."

"Go on alone then. Find some other sucker to pick you up."

"No, I want to stay with you."

His eyes burned and stung, a gauzy grey web work appearing on his peripheral vision. He signed them in, noticing that he'd written Mr. and Mrs. Humbert Humbert. He showered, turning the water on as hard and hot as he could stand it, but that didn't seem to affect the lethargy that was claiming him. When he came from the bathroom, his skin was tingling. Rue was on the bed, her hair bright against the pillow, the curtains of the open window drifting flimsily onto and off her body with its duskily freckled fair skin.

"I was foolish to try and run from them," she said with a welcoming gesture. "The worlds lie close, as close as we are to each other now."

In her arms he dreamed. He was stifling in a small, dim, odorous room. In the odd perspective of dreams he saw a face, wizened as a dried apple, the jaw immense, the brow foreshortened with two green gleams where eyes should be beneath a bristling line where two eyebrows grew together over the bridge of the nose. Two other figures moved behind the first, and he thought that one of them wore a gaudy flower-print dress. A glass beaker filled with purplish liquid bubbled over a blue flame. He watched as a hand as skinny as a bird-claw brought something small and futilely writhing and dropped it into the beaker. He thought the figures clustered close together to enjoy its struggles as it was boiled alive. A casket, broken and encrusted with mold, began to vibrate wildly, dark rotting fragments flaking off it. From it a skeleton, all discolored bone and dried sinew, was struggling to rise.

"Sister-Cindy, bring the pot," said one of the entities in a hysterical half-shriek, and an amorphous blur, growing taller as it came gliding, resolved itself into a witch-shape. It poured the still-steaming contents over the skeleton's grinning skull, the stuff melting down the bones like candlewax, clinging, and forming a human shape. A moment longer and he would recognize it.

He awoke with the curtains flapping above his head, the wind carrying the heavy, dusty smell of rain. Rue was gone, the door standing open. Thunder grumbled as he dressed, and when he left the cabin, the sky was full of sullen cloud. He saw no one. Behind the motel grew a scrub forest, thin trees already swaying in the storm wind. He called out for Rue but there was no answer. Thunder called again, with more authority, and the lightning cast an eerie glow over the trees. The further he went into the forest, the more sluggish his movements became, and at a certain moment he feared to turn and look at the motel because he had the sudden certainty that it wouldn't be there .

He caught a fleeting glimpse of two dark hunched figures in patchwork garments slipping through the trees carrying something that looked like a bundle of dry twigs wrapped in black rags. He tried to force his body forward but it was as if the atmosphere had grown thick and liquid and it was all he could do just to move his legs.

Then he saw Rue, standing in a small clearing. One moment her eyes met his, a kind of pleading in them, the next with eyes as blank as a doll's. Her skin gone translucently pale, she slumped to the forest floor. Then there were three clustering black shapes, some-times appearing human, sometimes not, crying out with raucous voices as their black-nailed skinny hands fastened themselves into Rue's flesh.

"You're selfish!" Rue's inert body was jerked back and forth as they contested it, limbs bobbed lifelessly.

"Wanted to steal our persona when we all swore to share it."

"It's mine. Let me wear it!" Talon-like hands tore gashes in white skin. When he tried to shout, his jaw seemed frozen. The dark struggling bodies blocked his vision, still tearing and shouting, "Mine, mine!"

Time was distorted; the lightning when it hit was like a streak of gold melting down the tree beside him. There was a great concus-sion; a huge door slamming between worlds, and he toppled to the forest floor and lay there stunned.

When he awoke there was a charred smell in the air, and fire still smoldered at the base of the split tree. On the grass and soaked into the rocky soil everywhere were darkly glistening patches that stained his fingertips red when he touched them, "Who'd have thought she'd have so much blood in her," his thoughts giggled. And bits of yellowish muscle tissue and mottled lengths of viscera, here and there a shattered fragment of bone. "And who'd have thought she had the g-" The contents of his stomach burned up his throat and were expelled onto the grass.

He knew that somehow, he must have gotten himself together long enough to escape the motel and to reach the city. He must have talked to someone to rent this cheap room in a moldering old building because he was here and the walls with their uncertain pat-terns of brown waterstains overlaying faded bouquets were the one reality he had. He rose and shuffled across the room, kicking aside an empty whiskey bottle (he couldn't remember drinking that, either). He squinted through the slats of discolored Venetian blinds and tried to estimate the time of day, but the sky was overcast, the wind pushing about grimy scraps of fallen leaves. Whatever the time, he was hungry, and he guessed he still had enough money left to buy a meal.

He went out into the semi-dark of the cramped hallway and began to descend the stairs. On the landing, where the stairs turned, he passed someone, perhaps another tenant, though he couldn't remember seeing her before—a very old lady in a shapeless black dress, her hand a brown-spotted moth hovering over the stair-rail. He could swear he didn't know her, but she looked at him lingeringly, and there was a gleam of green in each deep-set eye beneath a bristling thicket of eyebrow.

Small Magic

Old Ive's eyes darted nervously around the room as he entered. He had passed through ruined corridors where the webs of spiders trembled in the cold wind and vermin darted into crevices and crannies in the fallen stone where they had their nests. This inner chamber had all its walls intact; the flags of the floor were clean-swept and a modest fire burned on the hearth. One wall bore a tapestry in faded purple and gold—the hunt of the unicorn, though the edges were raveled and frayed.

He was a wizened old peasant with a sundark skin and a closed and suspicious expression. His first sight of the wisewoman had surprised him. He had known she was not old, but on first appearance she had seemed a mere girl with her hair loosely woven into a single plait, an odd, pale brown that in the firelight seemed the color of ashes, a loose gown of dun cloth making her body seem fragile and undeveloped. Yet now as the wisewoman faced him, standing in the firelight, he could not have called her a girl. Her eyes were a penetrating clear dark gray and the form beneath the gown had a tense vigor even in repose.

"They said . . . you were a weaver of spells," he said in a peevish rusty-gate voice as he continued looking her over with a surreptitious sidelong gaze.

Graye grew a trifle irritated with the old fool, and there was a muted thumping sound so that Old Ive looked frantically toward the door. "Soldiers," he said, in a strained voice.

"No." Graye smiled, an old joke with herself.

"Are you sure? The villagers have talked of naught for a month but the slaughter at TorCaerme, and they said the rebels were being harried in this direction by Lutin's men.

"Not soldiers—not this time," said the witch remembering idly when the armies of Prince Lutin had come through, reducing this place to the ruin it now was, killing all the male defenders including a father, a brother and two uncles. She had been taken to a hunting lodge in the hills with Aunt Maev, the fey one. There was only the memory, most of it at second hand for she had been young, not much pain, like an old scar, long-healed that one touches, from time to time in reassurance that it's still there. She realized that she had been staring blankly at Old Ive and forced herself to return to the present moment.

"They say you have Power," he was saying. He scrabbled among the folds of his grimy surcoat and slowly drew out a coin, thin and polished by much handling. He had Graye's interest, for the moment. Most of the villagers paid in baskets of grain or shoats. "I got me an enemy, lives next to me down past Runningwater. He's been a thorn in my side for years. Claims my fence is built over on his land. I want a curse on him, you know how to do it, a sickness . . . or maybe a fire." His pouched old face dwelt on the delicious possibilities.

The rapping began again, this time in the stones of the wall, mortar beginning to sift down in fine streams. Ive was lost in his hate and did not seem to notice.

"No, I can curse no one. My magic is small and peaceful. Herb teas, fortunes sometimes, unbinding."

"That," said the old man, spitting the word like a wad of phlegm, "is no magic at all." His eyes narrowed, filled with an ignorant malice. "So they were wrong about the Power. You're just a woman—like any woman." He stood there silently a moment as his slow mind dredged up other possibilities. He took a step toward her.

As he did, the tapping began again and objects on the table beside them began a sympathetic vibration. Graye pointed to the table, her eyes blank with concentration. A clay jar began to move, very slowly, as if it were something ponderous, inching its way across the scarred wood. Old Ive watched it with slack mouth and when it reached the edge and fell to shatter on the stones, he turned and scuttled away, calling querulously on the old gods to defend him. Graye looked down the drafty corridor to be sure that he had gone, then returned to her antique high-backed chair by the chimney corner and sank down exhaustedly. Aunt Maev had talked about this or that member of the family having the Power, as if they could change the course of rivers or move mighty mountains, but what had she done here—put to flight a poor ignorant peasant—what a use for the Power. She wasn't sure whether to laugh or cry about it, so she only sat there for some moments, holding her aching head in her hands.

Not many days later she was bringing some dried herbs into the village for barter when she noticed that few villagers were about, the cottages silent and closed in upon themselves. Crossing the square, silent and patterned in sunlight and shadow, she saw a village woman who had once come to her for a tonic.

"Goodwife, what is troubling this place?"

"Soldiers have been seen, the broken army of the one they called the Wolf of TorCaerme. The Prince is on his heels so both armies may pass this way, and since Branwynhouse is destroyed we have no protection. Perhaps you, with your Power—"

Graye smiled wryly. Didn't the woman know that if the village were invaded their wisewoman could only run and hide with the rest. "I'll do my best," she said ironically and was surprised to see that the woman looked somewhat reassured.

As she walked home under the burden of her sack of meal, she felt a sense of unease as she approached her dwelling. All was quiet, the jagged and fallen stones lightly furred with green moss, frost-touched creepers growing around and through the crumbling walls. She saw the archer out of the corner of her eye, just as he fired. If she had not seen him—

The arrow veered in midflight, swept past her with a hollow whistling. She heard the man curse at the miss, and she tried to mindgrip a stone at his feet and send it hurtling up at him, but her anger had made her over-reach herself and she only ended up with an agonizing headache, saw-toothed jags of silver moving on the edges of her vision.

He cursed again, stepping out into the open, approaching her without fear. "I could not see you well," he said breathlessly. "I fired not knowing you were a maid; thank the gods you were not killed." He was dressed roughly in a leather shirt topped with light mail. His clothing was grimy as if he'd traveled a long way, but beneath the armor and the grime, he seemed not much more than a boy, loose-jointed and coltish, the thin frizz of a blond beard on his jaws. "I'm scouting for Kyrellin; this is the house of the Brothers Branwyn, is it not?" He spoke gravely, with an authority he didn't quite yet command, as if war were a game he played at.

"It was. Now it's mine. What's left of it."

"I'll need food," he said. "I've ridden all day."

Having recovered from her headache, she led the way inside. The scout rummaged around, helping himself to some bread and apples, wolfing it all down, then looking around for more. Infected for the moment by his enthusiasm she helped him, finding a chunk of salt-meat she'd put away for lean times. "How did you know this was Branwyn?" she asked, amazed at his appetite.

He paused as he fed wood profligately into her fire, making a huge blaze. "Kyrellin is of a branch of that family; he thought to find allies here against the Prince. They are all gone, then?"

"All but me. He will find no allies here. Perhaps he should travel to the south. He might reach the mountains and—"

The young soldier grinned lazily. "Perhaps the Wolf of TorCaerme will want to hear the advice of an addle-headed wench." But he seemed very sleepy now that he had eaten, and he was almost dozing in her chair, with a satisfied look as if thinking that he had made a very successful invasion. It was too bad, thought Graye, that he couldn't rest after his long ride, but she needed a messenger herself.

The rapping sounds along the walls began, letting her know that her Power was returning a little. The soldier's eyes came open suddenly, and he saw her gesture toward the fire, and as if on command, it was leaping at him, showering him with sparks. He jumpd up, slapping at his clothing, backing away from her.

"Tell your commander that there is no aid for him here, and that he will find no kinsmen, only enemies." She had not finished speaking when the soldier gripped the door, crying out when he felt its thumping vibration and thrust himself through it.

"And if he does come here I'll—" She waited a moment to be sure he was gone before continuing. "I'll frighten him with noises and with tricks to scare children," she said, breaking into laughter that she had to admit was a trifle hysterical.

She had thought the waiting was bad, but when she saw mounted men appear through the trees, she wished for a twelvemonth of the waiting. She let fall the bucket back into the cistern with a hollow echoing splash that complemented the hollowness she felt inside.

The lead rider's horse stumbled as they reached the summit of her hill, then it groaned and sank down under him, lathered sides pumping. With a low oath the rider extricated himself from the tangled stirrups, drew a knife he carried at his belt and cut the beast's throat. Though it may have been a kindness, the distracted look of anger on his face made it seem more a revenge. What he looked like Graye couldn't tell because of the helmet, the beard and the grime, but she heard one of the others call him Kyrellin.

Having approached them silently and now only standing quietly among twilight's ballooning shadows, she managed to give the impression of almost, a materialization. There was a babble of perturbation, a few muttered curses, excited horses jerked their heads, caromed off each other. Kyrellin glanced up and then as if trying for effect himself, wiped the knife on the tail of a shirt so filthy it could not be further soiled. She saw that his hands were still stickily red between the fingers.

"She's the one young Olin spoke of," said one of the soldiers. "He called this a witch-house and said he feared to come back here."

Kyrellin shot him a look that silenced him. The others began to calm their mounts and to unsaddle and tend them in embarrassed si-

lence. "Olin lives up to his name," said Kyrellin. "Young . . . and untried." His voice was silken and soothing, a tone Graye did not
like—the purr of a tiger. He removed his helmet as he looked at the
ruin of the great dwelling and Graye remembered her aunt referring
to "that hawk-nosed Kharis branch of the family." A puckered scar
was aslant his right cheek and brought the corner of his lip up in a
permanent sneer.

"My father spoke of this place. A house to stand against storms,
he called it. I had hoped—" He seemed to come back to himself and
glared at her angrily as if she had been spying on his inmost
thoughts. "Is there no man in charge of the house?"

"As I told you, all died."

"Then perhaps that is why you neglect your duty and allow a
kinsman to stand outside in the cold air. A man is needed to set the
house to rights and I need a place to quarter my officers while we
regroup and plan strategy." As he spoke he was entering without
bothering to wait for her invitation, which never came in any case.

"It was a long run from TorCaerme; I don't even remember
what it is to be clean or full-fed or rested." He looked around the inner chambers she had made snug for her own habitation. "I want
water to wash with and food, lots of it—enough for all of us—hot."
A faint rattling vibration began in a corner of the ceiling but Kyr
hardly seemed to notice it.

"There have been no servants here for years," said Graye. "I've
become accustomed to fetching and carrying for myself."

"Good, then cousin, if kinswoman you truly are and not some
opportunist of a serving wench, you won't mind offering the hospi-
tality due me."

Grudgingly she found a large kettle and depleted her larder to
prepare stew enough for all and carried buckets till she was exhausted. She met one of Kyrellin's men in the corridor and saw that
he carried a huge cask, astream with cobwebs. "That's my father's—my wine," she said as she was shouldered aside spilling a half
pailful of water across her feet.

"And it had better be good," he grinned back at her.

"It's not wise to appropriate the possessions of the dead," she said in a toneless voice.

"Whatever it is they do in the shadowland, I don't think it's drinking," he said flippantly, beginning to notice her in a way she didn't like, "or for that matter—" A good-sized chunk of mortar was dislodged and fell close to him, making him sidestep in surprise and nearly drop the cask. He looked upward suspiciously.

"This is an old house," she said with a faint smile.

"What are you saying, that it's haunted?"

"I only said it was old," she replied, pushing past him to bring the water. A man shouted to be served and she ladled out stew, having threaded her way through half-clad bodies to deliver it. The man took hold of the bowl with one hand and put his other arm around her waist, attempting to drag her down onto his lap. He got only the boiling-hot stew as she mindgripped the bowl and tipped it neatly out. Dishes in a cupboard began a sympathetic rattling.

"What's the uproar," said Kyrellin, naked to the waist, heavily muscled, his chest sooty-dark with hair.

"She spilled soup on me," said the man, holding the steaming cloth of his trousers away from his skin.

"You're a clumsy fool," said another man. "I saw her; she never touched the bowl."

"Somehow, it seemed she did."

"You'd best be out of here," said Kyr and grasping her by the shoulder he steered her toward the door. She moved without speaking, like a sleepwalker. There was something about the touch of his hand, even through the homespun cloth of her gown. There was a humming sensation deep in her brain as of a force building power yet somehow dampened.

He pushed her out into the drafty corridor and slammed the door on her. It was strange but tipping the bowl should have drained her, yet it had not. She felt capable of more than she had ever tried before. But she would wait, for full dark and until they had drunk enough wine to distort even the smallest and most pacific magic into something frightening.

At full moonrise she knelt by the door and listened—loud brutish snores. She pushed back the door and saw the mounded shapes of the soldiers rolled into the blankets by the wan light of the dying fire. She mindgripped the blanket over a nearby sleeper and began to pull it out of his grasp. He sat up, wild-eyed, to see it like something alive sliding off his body to crouch in threatening folds and then jump back at him. By this time, knocking sounds were coming from all corners of the room and the man's full-throated shriek must have prickled the hair at the back of his comrades' necks. She edged two metal bowls off the table where they bounced and rolled, adding to the clamor.

"Witches!"

"The dead!"

She brought back the dying fire for a last hissing burst of bright flame. Half naked figures leaped about the room, firelight reddening their skin, and there was a general rush to the door which she barely avoided, being so intent on her work. She sent a blanket flapping and flopping after the last man to twine about his ankles and make him stumble into the wall.

Silence and darkness throughout the ruined dwelling, only the sour whine of the wind kept outside by the stout walls. The fire had been exhausted by that last burst of energy, and she felt her own Power now dissolved to ashes. She had done more than she had thought possible; she had stretched her small magic to its limits, and the enemy was gone. She bolted her door carefully even though she didn't think they would be back.

She gathered a handful of scattered kindling to revive the fire and dragged her pallet-bed near it in preparation for the night. She was not surprised now that weariness came at her in waves. She cast off the hampering homespun gown, stretched her lean, compactly muscled body in the fire's warmth, undid the strange, no-color hair, translucent in the red light and brushed it, while she tried to remember the words to an old tune. She couldn't remember them; stopped singing and chuckled to herself. "Well, cousin, it's a pity you couldn't stay to lay your plans, but no strategy is needed for a retreat."

Off in a corner something moved, a darkness darker than the shadows around it; then it detached itself from shadow and shambled forward.

"A retreat, cousin, but not a rout." Kyrellin did not stand quite steadily, and his eyes were bleary from drink, but his voice was still a tiger's purr. "My family talked about the blood of the Branwyn's being tainted by witchcraft. My mother herself had a little of the Power—like that wall tapping that panicked my superstitious officers."

Graye reached for a mindgrip and got nothing, not even a vibration from loose objects in the room. She shivered and wrapped a blanket around herself, but Kyrellin continued to stand just in the shadow beyond the firelight and continued to talk with a deceptive calmness. "The day my mother died a stool flew across the room and smashed to kindling against the wall. I heard the rapping and pretended not to notice it. I baited you, hoping to find out what you could do, but you waited, biding your time until the dark magnified the terror of the unknown. You used your resources well, but they are at an end."

"You don't know that, unless you're gifted as well with the second sight."

"I know it because you're afraid of me and if you could have done anything to me you'd have done it by now." He drew closer, his face swimming out of the darkness as he sat down beside her on the pallet. "You'd be dead now, I think, except that when you took off your garment before the fire, I remembered an old hunger—a man's hunger. You understand." As he spoke he was unwinding the blanket from around her shoulders, pulling it out of her numb hands. And as his fingertips happened to brush her arm, she became aware of a resonant humming deep within her skullbones as of some incomprehensible power building. She had been half hypnotized by the flicker of the fire and his quiet voice, but now she drew away.

"Don't touch me," she said through dry lips. "Something is going to happen."

"Yes," he said with a smile the scar pulled into a leer. "Something is." He pushed her roughly backward, and the moment they touched, she felt the energy build to an unbearable tension. From this moment she understood what Aunt Maev had meant when she said The Power. Kyrellin was giving her an earful of barracks language as he mauled her breasts, when even he began to realize that, as she had said, something was happening. The stones of the walls and ceiling were beginning to vibrate, sending down showers of mortar, and there was a cool, blue other-worldly light in the room.

"We've got to get out of here," shrieked Graye, trying to pull away from him, but he clung to her with a stunned expression as the stones of the wall began to dance wildly and to fall from their places. When a huge stone smashed down beside him, he let go all holds and raced her for the door. Graye was pushed aside but managed to get out just as the ceiling collapsed with a roar. When they had run out into the dooryard and collapsed into a tangle of dew-wet grass and nightblooming flowers, they began little by little to realize that there was to be no more destruction. The ruin still stood in the moonlight like a carious tooth, dust beginning to settle.

"You had me in the palm of your hand the whole time," said Kyrellin. "And yet you waited until—"

"I could have crushed you with a falling stone, had I chosen." Her voice shook, but she pretended it was with cold. "Get me something to put on." She waited breathless to see how he would take to a direct order, but he still seemed a little stunned and cast about until he found a shirt discarded by one of his fleeing men. He was about to put it around her shoulders. "No. Just toss it here."

"You brought down walls and ceiling; the walls shuddered . . . and fell."

She shrugged. "My control was poor, I admit, but—"

"Don't you know that Prince Lutin sits behind his high walls at Lastegarde and thinks himself safe. And the four Unconquerable Baronies of the Plain, his minions. If you could but stand outside those walls and call down your power."

"So you could butcher the inhabitants? I've had enough of falling walls for one night. Do you think you could make us a fire in what's left of my house?" Angrily he stalked off but after a moment she saw him gathering tag ends of fallen branches. She did not think she should try to push him any further. In the morning, unless she told him the truth, he would ride away. And the Power would go with him. She would be safe, safe to go back to living by her wits and deceiving the innocent and ignorant. That had always been good enough before. Still it was hard not to speculate about what it would be like to have real power. Before she could come to any clear decision, she slept.

The following morning Graye inspected the damage to her house, and in doing so, climbed a crumbling staircase to the top of the one tower still standing. She stood looking out over the countryside, trees foliaged in umber, apricot and dull dry-blood color, the whole scene washed grayly with morning fog. The roof of the tower had long ago fallen in, and she felt the damp chill as the fog condensed into droplets. She had not stood here in a long time, and she had forgotten what a proprietary feeling it was to look over Branwynlands.

The sound of footsteps on the stairs startled her. "You shouldn't have come up here. The staircase might have broken under your weight."

Kyrellin ignored her and looked out over the landscape. The light had shifted and objects began to show through the aura of fog with sharp-edged reality. "Proud lands," he said. "Your house and all these grounds could be restored if you would agree to use your power against Lutin. I've thought about it until my head aches and I can't understand why you would not strike, having the Power in your hand. Have you grubbed with peasants so long that you've lost all sense of family pride, that you would let the Red Prince and his minions laugh at your father's memory?"

"That is an old war. I was young—and knew my father hardly at all. If the dead cry for revenge, I don't hear them."

"A frightened, whey-faced, whining woman," he shouted.

That should have been funny, but somehow she did not find it so, though she knew that by refusing to answer, she would be slamming shut a door on his anger. As though unbidden the words came, "I don't believe you found me so easy to frighten—last night." Too late to take back the words, she realized that he was so unused to being baited that he would react only with violence. He grabbed her wrist and twisted it, and at his touch the stones of the tower groaned, ground together, the landscape lurching unsteadily in the slotted window.

"Let go," she said, clawing at his hand as she felt the tower lean outward. "You'll kill us both!"

The stones grew still and the lands around resolved themselves, but there was an air of unsteadiness about the ancient tower. Kyrellin looked at his hand, seeming to take forever to make the connection. "It wasn't you. It was us? Together?"

"We've got to get down from here. The tower is dangerously weak." A certainty dawning, he reached toward her and she had to cringe away.

"Not just your magic? When we touch, mine as well."

"Yes, damn you, do you want us both to die here?"

"I want to—Well, let's get out of this place first." The stairs shuddered as they eased their way down, and when they had reached the bottom, a gust of wind caught the tower and sent it hurtling outward from the wall. "You meant to let me ride away, not knowing."

"I don't know."

"But now you'd disavow it because I'm a part of the bargain. It's all out of your hands now. I will ride against Lastegarde, and whether you like it or not you will ride with me."

Graye moved about, trying to find a comfortable position in the saddle, but there wasn't one; it seemed the journey was one long ache, but at least they had slowed to a walk. In the dust-whitened men's clothing she wore and with her long hair cut off she felt anonymous among the riders. That had been Kyrellin's idea, and it made sense, but she still faintly angered, since she suspected it was because he didn't want it generally known that a woman rode with him. There was a commotion ahead and she saw men pointing toward rugged hills that were like folds in some coarse golden cloth. Sun glinted blueblack off a structure atop the highest hill, the fort of Wellain. She shaded her eyes to look at it. "It glistens so; is it of glass?"

"They light fires and burn the clay as the wall is built; it gives the material great strength," said Olin who held the rein of the small-boned sorrel she rode. "I wish I knew more of Kyrellin's plan. A frontal assault on Wellain's walls sounds like folly to me."

As they rode, the walls before them drew upward to a great height. They could see archers moving along the parapet, and hear their faint voices calling down jibes and obscenities. Kyrellin came to take the rein from Olin. "Now will the Power be tried."

Graye clung to the saddle as he urged his horse into a trot. "There are archers up there with drawn weapons. What if we were mistaken about the Power?"

An arrow struck the earth a few feet in front of them.

"After seven years of throwing my armies against these invincible walls—this," said Kyrellin disgustedly. He reached over to grasp her hand and stirrup to stirrup they rode toward the walls.

"They're going to fire on us."

"You'll get used to it."

"I don't want to get used to it."

The jeers of those along the top of the wall died as the vibration began to work its way up through the vitrified material. They let loose a rain of arrows, but the brittle glaze of the surface was radiating hairline cracks, flakes of its substance slithering down its sides. Then a whole section broke free and came down. By this time the remainder of Kyrellin's army had moved up, and waited as the substance of the wall was rent and was crumbling to powder around its agonized defenders.

Kyrellin threw the rein to Olin again. "Get her out of here." Graye clung to the saddle as the sorrel struck up a lope behind Olin's gelding. From the summit of one of the cloth-fold hills they watched Kyrellin's army overwhelm the defenders, already stunned and half buried in the debris of their walls. "I knew you were a witch," said Olin, "but this—"

"I did nothing; it was all Kyrellin's work. And if you don't mind, I don't want to watch." She slid to the ground and walked down into a sheltered vale. Olin seemed loath to give up his view of the battle, but after a moment he followed her. "I wasn't running away. Watch the killing if you enjoy it."

"No, I have my orders," he said rather regretfully. She sat down with her back toward him in a path of tall grass, angry that he could play at soldier with such appalling innocence, but when she looked over her shoulder and saw that he was standing guard over her like a sentry, she realized that the innocence would soon be gone; soon enough he would lose his illusions, and perhaps such a loss should not be taken lightly.

"Can't you sit down, at least, jailer? You're making me nervous." He sensed that she was mocking him and stood his ground for a few moments, but after awhile she heard the grass rustle and felt his shoulders graze hers as he sat.

"It's so quiet here, it could just be the two of us out for a walk, or—" Olin made a slight, disgusted sound. Closing her eyes, she lay back, causing the grass to whisper and give off a pungent spice-smell, and upon opening them she saw Olin looking down at her. "Well," she said, stretching her arms upward so the rough cloth of the shirt outlined her breasts. "I suppose you're still sulking about all the glory you're missing out on."

"No, I'm thinking that you're making fun of me, thinking I'm young and ignorant . . . maybe even virginal." He moved closer and shifted his weight so that he could bend down more closely. "And I'm thinking that you might find out the opposite, much to your surprise," he said, beginning in gruff soldierly tones that softened as he began to grin. "Only—"

"Kyrellin," she said, finishing the thought. "That bastard intrudes everywhere. I can't protect you from him if he finds out."

"Protect me?" said Olin exasperatedly. "I'm the jailer here." She laughed warmly and drew his weight against her.

With the threat of Kyrellin almost an actual presence their coupling was hasty, reckless, almost desperate, and a feeling of hatred for her situation blocked her pleasure, made the act almost mechanical. "Not so easy," she thought, watching him sleep in the nest of dried grass, "to recapture innocence."

She didn't know how long they had lain there when she heard the thump of hooves on the hard ground and a horse and rider topped the hill. Her first thought was of Kyrellin and she shook Olin roughly, but as the horseman drew near, riding very close upon them so that they had to look up at him as they rearranged their rumpled clothing, they saw with relief that it was only a messenger. He grinned down at them knowingly and addressed Olin.

"Wellain has fallen while you—slept. Kyrellin has sent me to say that he would be glad of her company at the evening meal."

From the look of the Great Hall, it was hard to tell that a struggle had taken place. Almost all was in order except for a decorative urn lying broken in a corner. On a dais a huge table was laden with food and watched over by a harried-looking servant who must have been left behind by the former inhabitants. Kyrellin sat drinking from a gold-chased cup, taking his ease at the head of the table as if he were rightful lord here. It should have been a cheering sight, for she was tired and hungry, but in the streets she had passed through, she had seen soldiers looting deserted dwellings, setting fires in the streets, reeling drunkenly about. Though she had been conducted here by a special route, she had seen one corpse, eyes turned back whitely, hands clutching emptiness, a smear of blood across belly and groin.

She forced herself to concentrate on where she was instead and saw that Kyrellin wore an unfamiliar garment, dark and rich with winking threads of silver worked through it. He made a welcoming gesture toward the table and indicated the chair beside him. "All this is ours to enjoy." He drank rapidly, noisily from the goblet as if he would drown himself in it.

"I want none of it."

Kyrellin shrugged and went on eating. The pungent smells of the food made her feel dizzy. After a time she sat down at the far end of the table and took food with the air of one who steals it, eating quickly. They ate in silence, not a festive meal despite the richness of the surroundings. Kyrellin continued to drink deeply.

"Now let them run to Lutin with the news that the Wolf has returned," he said. "Let them be afraid."

"Don't vaunt to me," she said pushing her chair back with a violence that overturned it. "Hiding behind magic to play your dirty games." He walked unsteadily toward her, hand lifted as if to strike. "Are you certain you want to touch me—suppose your hands fastened on my throat and you found yourself unable to let go in your rage?"

He paused, his hands falling lifelessly. He looked around at the walls, knowing they would fall and crush them both. "And even if you killed me, the Power is destroyed. So it seems the only freedom I have left is the freedom to say what I like, and you will control your anger, or choke on it."

He threw the golden cup and swore so loud and vile an oath that the servant darted behind a wall-hanging. Graye held her breath, having no idea what would happen next, but when a moment had passed without violence, she began to feel hope.

"Let me go. Nothing good can come of this alliance."

Kyrellin's voice was low, but the outburst seemed to have cleared his mind.

"You know I can't."

"Since I can be no further use to you tonight, call my jailer. I'm feeling tired."

He sat down, signaled the poor servant to replace the cup he'd thrown from him. She didn't like the look of calculation that had replaced the bleary drunkenness. "I named young Olin to that post, did I not? Young, yes, but perhaps not so untried as once he was. I'm told he has grown to enjoy his duties."

She shrugged. "Perhaps. But it was you who gave him power over me."

"It's not *his* power over you that worries me."

She smiled, slowly and unpleasantly. "Why should you care? You can't touch me, in any case."

"Yes, I remember. You are safe . . . in the eye of the storm. I wonder . . . do you know of a man in my army who is called Hamel? Hamel the Boar he is called. Not a very handsome specimen, I suppose, but he considers himself quite handy with the ladies."

She visualized the man he spoke of, heavy, swarthy, vaguely distorted with his head slightly twisted on his short, thick neck, small porcine eyes close-set and gleaming. "Think of him as your jailer. If I can't touch you, he can, and I would be glad to suggest amorous games to him if his imagination were to fail."

Her voice caught in her throat when she tried to speak. "You would not," she managed to stammer at last.

He smiled but it was with a haggardness that showed how weary he was of the day's fighting. "Of course I would. Think of that before you make yourself disagreeable again."

A corpse lay white and naked in a heap of blackened shards, the skin a little bloated. One of his eyelids had been eaten away by vermin, leaving the eyeball bulging obscenely. As Graye sat among the ruins, she heard a rustling in the debris and looked to see the hand of the corpse scrabbling for a purchase on broken stone. She watched horrified as it began to inch forward, wormlike, pulled by first one clutching hand and then the other, the swollen face lolling to one side. The jaw had dropped loosely and from the darkly open mouth came a single echoing word,

"You—oo—oo."

She scrambled to one side of the bed in a convulsive movement, tangled smotheringly in the bedcurtains, fought free and lay there trembling in the dark. She kept herself from crying out to Olin who was outside her door because she was afraid she would see Hamel slouching in through the door in answer to her call. After a few minutes she struggled free of the bedclothes and stood in the chill moonlight of the bedchamber. It was practically empty, having been cleared out by the fleeing family and then looted by Kyrellin's men. She went to the door and listened—gentle snores—Olin asleep at his post. She pushed against the door, already knowing it was barred from the outside.

Driven by memory of the dream she estimated the position of the bar and tried to get her mind around it. She heard it move against the door, old, dry, light wood, but in the use of the greater Power the lesser had atrophied. She moved the bar a little further, her head throbbing. She forced herself, thinking that those snores in the corridor might be Hamel's in a few days. She was clammy with sweat when the bar slid back enough to let the door swing free; she had just enough strength left to go through it.

The chill air cleared her head as she set out, walking among rocky hills gleaming with frost under the moon's witch-light. There was a village huddled beside the fort's broken walls, but she avoided that, and beyond, the land was barren and thinly settled. She was at first only anxious to put as much distance as she could between herself and Kyrellin, but when the sun rose, she began to think of such necessities as food and water. There was ice here and there trapped in the hollows of rocks, liquefying as the sun rose, but all the food she found were some half dried berries in a stand of spidery black bushes. The plant lore passed on by Aunt Maev judged these as edible so she stopped for a sparse meal.

Evening's light picked her out sharply on the barren terrain, a lone figure still moving with some strength, though that was waning. The wind was cold. She huddled in the lee of a cairn of rocks piled up by earlier peoples to mark who knew what feat of valor. She knew she would have to find real food tomorrow, or her journey would end before it was well begun. She wondered why she hadn't stolen provisions before leaving, or a horse, but it was too late for such regrets. If she managed to reach another settlement, her small magic would convince the villagers to give her food and lodging; it seemed odd to have to rely on those old tricks. She stood looking out over the barren, rock-strewn landscape for some time, as if deciding whether or not to travel on.

She was still standing there when she saw four mounted men top the ridge above her. That they began to shout and lash their horses told her she had been seen. She began to run, dodging patches of loose rock and straggling stands of brush. If she could get over the next hill there was a chance she might find a hiding place in the broken terrain. When she paused at the crest of the hill, her breath wheezing, an open meadow of dry grass stretched away before her. Without any reason except habit she continued to run, but the dulled sound of hoofbeats across turf built from behind and the sweat-gleaming bay shoulder of a galloping mount blurred into her vision to one side, passed by, the rider reining sharply in front of her. She was so tired she didn't know why she didn't fall, but she stood holding her side and trying to breathe as the other riders joined the first. She. didn't know their names but she had seen some of them before.

Looking around she saw that her last burst of speed had brought her very near an eroded outcropping of rock, crowned with several boulders. She edged toward it.

"Is this the witch?" asked the man on the bay. He had a round, ruddy face and a great deal of curling hair spilling out from the edges of his helmet.

"This is the one," said a gaunt man whose uniform fit like clothes on a scarecrow.

"Stand away," she said. "You know I have Magic."

The red faced man slid down from his horse. "This witch is too saucy; I'll have to teach her to defer to her betters."

"Touch me and I'll have these stones down around your ears," she said and made a theatrical gesture toward the boulders that balanced so precariously. The ruddy man backed away so rapidly he caught his foot on a branch and fell.

The others laughed uproariously an the gaunt man spurred his horse in close to Graye and reached down to hoist her up behind him when he realized that nothing was going to fall on him.

Graye was stunned for a moment or two and then realized that instead of using her own magic to roll down a pebble or two and

perhaps startle them enough to make her escape, she had attempted
to bring down the larger stones.

It was dawn by the time they returned to the Hall. Light from
nearly melted candles in high sconces did nothing but nibble tim-
orously at the heavy gloom of the place, and Kyrellin half drowsing
in a tall chair seemed a part of that gloom. "You didn't find it so easy
to escape me," he said, almost an anonymous voice from where he
sat, half in shadow. But the voice was flat, emotionless .

"What I was running from, no one escapes," she said.

"I don't trust you when you admit defeat."

"I don't. It's just that something is settled, that's all. Time moves
only from the known into the unknown, though not always without
some struggle, some irrevocable loss."

"I liked you better when you argued; these riddles are beyond
me and there's nothing amusing about them." He cleared his throat
nervously. "In any event I'll be rid of you soon. Tomorrow we ride
on Lastegarde."

"Then it is you who will renounce the Power, and the Wolf of
TorCaerme will take up the shepherd's staff. Pardon me, but I doubt
it."

"Do you think I loved hauling you along all this time, swallow-
ing your insults. Don't you think I'm tired of hearing about your innocence and my guilt?"

She nodded. "You're right. Responsibility must be the first
step."

"The first step to what—damn you!"

"To control."

"You control nothing here. I make the terms. I can send you to
your cell, I can choose your jailer, visit on you any indignities I
please."

She was silent.

"Speak up, is that not true?" She did not have to speak. Both of
them knew it was true and also, that now it didn't matter.

The walls of Lastegarde rose from morning mists as if they floated on clouds. The sorrel moved at a lope and now Graye managed to follow the movement without thinking. Though before she had accompanied Kyrellin in a state of numb horror, today things interested her. She wondered what the men along the top of the wall were thinking. They didn't jeer or toss down bits of debris as those in the other forts had. She could imagine what tales had ben passed along until they had grown out of all proportion.

When she approached Kyrellin she saw that he was in heated conversation with his highest ranking officers. He looked angry when he mounted as if he were, for once, accepting counsel from others, but doing it grudgingly. His huge black horse grabbed at the bit and he jerked back on the reins, making the monster half rear, rolling white-rimmed eyes. The walls grew more solid out of co-cooning mists, sunlight a wall of polished brass behind them. A desultory arrow struck the dust ahead of them. Graye didn't think the defense would be wholehearted. Perhaps Lutin and his family had already fled.

Olin tossed the sorrel's rein to Kyrellin and he looked at it and then at her in a distracted way. "Lastegarde," he said, "just beyond the reach of my hand. If you could understand how I've held this moment before me, a lamp to scatter shadows when they lay deep."

"Let those walls fall then," she said. "For my murdered kinsmen, if vengeance is truly what the dead want." She held out her hand, but Kyrellin refused to take it.

"You don't want vengeance or sovereignty or lands or anything as wholesome as that. You want the Power for its own sake."

"I want to know it, if it's a part of me. All we gave to it was our mutual hatred. We won't know if it's capable of more than pure destruction until we've tested it."

"And in your testing, if you took us both in to the dark and lost us there?" She did not answer and with an oath he tossed the rein to her. "You're no longer chained to the beast-lord. I give you your freedom. At least leave me the dignity of fighting as a man fights."

Since nothing was happening the archers on the wall began to fire, raising a thin cheer when one of their shafts nearly found its mark.

The gates are opening," shouted a soldier. "They've become impatient with us; they're sending out their forces."

"Don't be a fool," said Graye. "It's not in your nature any more than in mine to settle for what is safe and familiar through fear alone."

She thrust out her hand again, not knowing what would come of this alliance, not even needing to know. Kyrellin didn't look happy about it, but light was glinting off the arms of a troop massing just beyond the opened gate. He joined hands with her. Before them was a rending noise, shrill shouts, confusion. Walls were beginning to come down.

In the Kingdom of the Thorn

It was not a pleasant land that she rode through; the hoofs of her broad-chested Hyksos warhorse brought up veils of fine grit. In most places the yellow soil was dried in geometric patterns, and thorny creepers spiraled across it at intervals. Here and there a reddish patch of vegetation held its own against the arid land. She had not expected to find a human soul in this wasteland, so it was a surprise when she saw a group of figures ahead. Heat blurred and distorted their outlines, but she saw the shapes of three horses and of four men and caught sight of a green garment.

She was uncertain whether to draw nearer when she saw the green-appareled figure go down among those more darkly dressed, and she saw a fist rise and fall. Old instincts drew her, and the group ahead froze into a tableau as she shouted a war-cry, drew the strangely dull-blue blade at her side and jammed spurred heels into the warhorse's sides.

Taken by surprise the assailants were almost under the pounding hooves before they could draw steel. One, without drawing a weapon, turned and ran for his horse; one stood his ground, aiming his weapon upward toward the gelding's throat. She rode the swordsman down; once the big beast built up momentum there was no way to stop him quickly, even if she'd wanted to, but once past, he set his feet and swung around, as he'd been trained, to make another charge.

She met the remaining man sword to sword, the shock of it sending a tremor through her well-muscled arm. It was too awkward handling the reins at the same time, so when she had a chance, she kicked her leg over the pommel and slid to the ground. She soon realized that he was no trained swordsman, though he was a head taller and had a better reach. As he cut at her again, she caught his sword on the edge of her slate-blue steel and his weapon broke.

He looked more embarrassed and angry, she thought, than fearful as she backed him up with the point of her weapon. He had a scruffy, sandcolored untrimmed beard and wore greasy leather clothing. A robber, or renegade, she decided.

"You wear no insignia," he said. "Yet, I think—"

"I wear no insignia because I have none."

"But you are an Amazon by the beast you ride and the way you wield a sword."

The man in green moaned and stirred.

"Return what you have stolen from this man and I will let you go."

"He had nothing to steal. He is some fanatic wandering the waste for his own inscrutable purposes. I had heard the Amazons took no prisoners."

"I never claimed to be of that bloody tribe," she said. "Now go, before I decide they have a point."

She set the literal point firmly into his chest, but he did not run. He walked insolently toward his horse. When he was safely mounted, he called back. "You may live to regret your decision; Arjen does not take defeat lightly."

The traveller in the short green robe had regained his feet, and she saw that he was slight of build, yet strikingly handsome with long curling hair into which was wound a garland of leaves. He wiped the blood from his swollen lips and shouted as he saw the robber riding away. "You let him go? Why did you not slay the transgressor? If the Seed be struck down before the planting, what shall come of the Harvest?"

Feeling that he was becoming incoherent, she went to him and made him sit down. She brought her water bag from the saddle, gave him a drink and cleaned the blood from his face.

"I thank you," he said, more calmly. "I did not mean what I said before. My way is a way of Peace and Gentleness."

As he looked at her, she saw that his eyes were a peculiar shade of hazel that gave the impression of light shining through green leaves in a forest glade. "My name is Dendros the Gardener."

"When I gave away my armor, I tried to break the sword as well, but it is daemon-forged; it will not break. Though it gained me another enemy today, I'm glad there was a weapon to hand when I needed one. My battle-name is Scorpia, and I have not yet considered another."

"I thank you for saving my life, which is, of course, worthless except for the Keeping of the Seed. I was on my way to the village Hetsepp where I hoped to inspire a Gathering."

"With the kind of riffraff spawned by these barren hills, perhaps I should accompany you. Meeting a man of peace seems propitious since I have sworn to give up war." After resting a little longer, Scorpia walked along in the dust of the road with the cultist, the warhorse trailing behind on a loose rein, and they talked quietly, as they walked. There was something about his voice and aspect that was as a splash of cool water on dying grass. As if by a miracle the drylands gave way to country thinly grown with brittle and stunted foliage, then to land green and thickly grown. The river that provided this bounty showed a small collection of mud-brick structures along its bank. "Do you mind," began Scorpia as they paused beside one of these clumsy dwellings, "if I stay to see the Gathering you spoke of?"

"If you wish."

In the heat of late afternoon the leaves of the trees hung dusty and limp. Adults went sluggishly about their business while the children of the place played in and out of the sun and shadow. As a boy and girl went running across a clearing between buildings, Dendros whistled sharply. The boy froze and the girl darted behind a tree bole to look out, big-eyed. Dendros motioned toward himself and stood quietly as the two youngsters came to stand self-consciously before him. Their skinny, browned arms and legs emerged from sack-like garments. "I have come for the Gathering," said Dendros, and they looked at him, shiny-eyed and solemn. "You must help me in the name of the Seed. Go, find the children of the village; tell them I would speak to them here, in this clearing." Like sprites they disappeared among the trees. They might have been frightened off, or might yet be, among the leaves, giggling at the man who talked to them so foolishly.

"They are but children," said Scorpia. "Should you not save your wisdom for those who can appreciate it?"

"You laugh at me," said Dendros, "and think the children understand nothing, but believe me, they understand, and there will be a Gathering. We need only wait."

Scorpia smiled, fastening her tawny hair more securely under the fillet. "I think," she said, "that a man who devotes himself to children is strange . . . yet wonderful."

A short time later they came whistling through the trees like birds, or appeared at one side of the clearing as lean and timid as deer, or came giggling and pushing each other. They came until there was a Gathering of about fifteen children, ranging in age from a tall, lanky almost-man to a toddler dragged by an older sister.

Scorpia stood back amazed as Dendros gathered the children into a circle around himself. After a moment, she went to sit among them, without embarrassment, as if she were a child herself. Dendros did not talk foolish talk to them as she had often heard other adults do. He told them of the Garden of the Shining Seed over which he was the Gardener. He told of bountiful water dripping down and of rich greenness that was seldom seen in this land. He told of perfect peace and contentment and promised eternal life in the name of the Garden and of the Seed. When he had finished, the Amazon, the sword-wielder, could almost believe it was possible. The children rose and some of them cheered and others embraced him.

"We will leave by night, in secrecy," said Dendros. "You must leave your families without a word. This is much to ask, and perhaps all may not find themselves ready for such a journey, but if anyone mentions me or the Garden, you will wither like a leaf in a furnace. And Die."

Scorpia almost believed this, too, but a faint suspicion stirred. There was a frightening light in Dendros's eyes. When the children were gone the two of them walked in deeper shade along the river's edge. When they paused, Scorpia touched Dendros's hand, but instead of being hot with blood, it was cool as grass gorged with dew. "You are not," she said, "as other men."

"No." He traced a hairline scar along her jaw with cooling fingertips.

"I don't care that you are not," she said. "One who knows the peace that I see on your face—in your eyes, cannot be evil. I have sworn to give up the sword, but I have had difficulty. Perhaps you could help me."

"You are strong and beautiful, and I owe you my life, but it is a Garden of Children that I tend. For you it is too late."

When she heard this Scorpia turned away, for it seemed now that she would never be able to change, to give up violence forever. She felt an arm cool as grass stalks slipped around her waist. "The Seed may not prosper in the head of a person fully grown. I received the Seed myself when I was no more than twelve."

"I understand. You are creating a world of harmony, and only the children have not been touched by the violence of our world. I have a gift for you, to show that you have changed me." She slipped the gray-blue sword from its sheath and put it in his hands.

"I wish I were a proper man—to please you."

She squeezed his hand, but thought now that she did not like the dry, chalky feel of his flesh. "That's no problem, or if it is, it's mine. Fare well on your way to the garden."

Wings of moths, duskily translucent, battered against the fading daylight, and she knew it was time for the Gathering and time for her to find lodging, if that were possible, for the night. She walked back to the mud-brick buildings and was passing along a narrow pathway between the structures when the charger she led made a sudden backward lunge, too late to alert her of the man who stepped from the doorway behind her and dragged her backward into ill-smelling darkness. The bone of his forearm bit into her windpipe until swimming black shapes blurred her vision. For a moment she couldn't imagine the cause of such an attack, if indeed cause were necessary. She scrabbled for a sword where no sword was. She briefly wondered what peace-loving people did in a case like this.

"Arjen made you a promise, lion-hair, and one he means to keep directly. Stop that, or I'll choke you into unconsciousness again. That's better. He told me to detain you here until he had taken care of the charlatan in the green robe. But you are not so ugly as he said you were; I may decide not to wait for him." He talked on, only a disembodied voice and a moist warm breath on the back of her neck. His free hand slid over her body familiarly. She pulled her attention back as she heard him say, "I had to laugh at Arjen when he said you bested him at swords. That made him angry; he said you had an enchanted blade. Where is it? Your scabbard is empty."

She fought to speak, her voice a croak. "It's on my saddle, but you could not wield it."

He laughed, pulling her arm up behind her and pushing her toward the doorway. She readied herself. One chance would be all. A spurred heel gashed the calf of the robber's leg and she tore free of his grip as he inhaled raspingly in pain. She dodged away down the alley to where the tall warhorse still stood. The way was very narrow; she barely had room to squeeze past the huge body, but as she did, she hit the gelding on the rump and shouted a loud command.

The robber stood transfixed with fear as the hooves pounded toward him. He slipped a dagger from its sheath, but the blade only deflected off the bone of a bluff shoulder, and he went down with an awful scream.

"Peace," said Scorpia, like a curse, and sidestepped the broken and bleeding form. She knew she had to protect Dendros if she could. Perhaps it was too late for her to turn from the ways of war, but not too late for the children.

It was difficult to find out which direction the band had taken, for those children who remained in the village were too frightened to tell. The nearly grown boy was the one to tell her at last, saying angrily that he had been left behind because he was too close to adulthood to join the Gathering.

She rode through the night and toward morning, found them camped in a stand of trees, the children sleeping peacefully while Dendros sat watching over them and staring into the fire. He kept his composure when she came pounding into the camp and set the big horse sliding to a stop. Somewhere was the sound of a child's frightened wailing, then it silenced as if another child had comforted him.

"You are all right?"

"Of course we are."

"Where is my sword?"

Dendros stood, his expression angry. "Why are you here? None is to know the location of the Garden."

"I'm sorry," she said, feeling like a scolded child, and yet another part of her mind wondered at how he could make her feel that way. She explained about the robber Arjen and complained, "If only I had slain him when I had the chance, as is thought proper among the Amazons."

"It seems the Seed still needs your protection," said Dendros, handing back her sword. "But if you accompany me to the Garden, you must promise never to leave."

They traveled across more desert, through inhabited lands, arriving at last in the stony foothills of an immense mountain range. There was a temple complex atop a boulder strewn ridge where the wind was a constant torrent. The architecture of the crumbling temples was odd, the structures high and narrow, the doorways small, as if humans were not really meant to pass through them. There were constructions inside whose functions had either been weathered away by time, or were incomprehensible to begin with. The central building was conical, very tall, and appeared to be roofless. A squat iron-banded door blocked the doorway. Before it the party paused, a brisk wind blowing the cornsilk hair of the children. They looked haggard from the hard journey, yet they looked up at Dendros with bright, trusting eyes.

"They may enter, but you may not," he told Scorpia. She strained her eyes to see as the door swung inward, but there was only a spiraling corridor of blank gray stone.

Languidly, she set up a camp, tethering and rubbing down the Hyksos steed, breaking out rations. She stood guard for some time, half expecting Dendros and the children to return, yet they did not, so she rolled into her blanket and slept.

When she awoke she found Dendros sitting and staring at her out of his strange eyes with the color of forest twilights in them.

"I stood guard almost until morning," she said, "yet Arjen has not appeared."

"You have been loyal. It is sad—"

"Sad?"

"I mean sad that you may not enter into the Garden, even though you have served the Gardener well."

"I will never see it?"

"You may not see it, yet perhaps you might be permitted entrance, with a blindfold, to experience the wonder of the place."

She allowed him to tie on the blindfold and to lead her through the groaning, iron-bound door. There was something unsettling in the way the door slammed to behind them, but she tried to shrug that off. They wound around the corridor and entered through another doorway. She sensed they were in a large room. The organic smell was incredible; it washed over her in tides of greenness. Water dripped somewhere with a cool plip-plop sound; never in this thorny land had she sensed such a surge of growth, such a feeling of perfect peace. Dendros pulled a frond of whatever grew here and let her feel the cool, lacy texture of it across her cheek. "I could stay here forever," she said.

"Perhaps you can, in a sense," came the voice of Dendros.

And then there was another voice, harsh, rasping, saying the crudest obscenities in the most hushed, awed voice she'd ever heard. Dendros was shrieking in anger and Scorpia tore the blindfold from her eyes. Light blinded her; it was pouring down from above, but it was no natural light. Something in the ceiling rendered it shifting, prismatic. She saw Arjen the robber, but he looked ashen, shaken to his foundation, then she turned to see what was affecting him so.

There, in a series of crystalline vats, were the children, their harnessed bodies hanging in the clear water. Their eyes were open, but not aware, and from time to time one of their mouths moved, as if saying a silent word, but the worst was behind and beyond them. There, perhaps a hundred children, row on row, were all in some stage of a strange growth. White rootlets protruded from open mouths, thorny vines and lacy fronds emerged from eye sockets, and waved lazily in the windless interior of the Garden. The farther back in the ranks, the more wasted were the bodies, the more skeletal the limbs, yet all moved with a dreamy writhing movement.

Scorpia felt her stomach contract, bent to retch dryly for a few moments. When she had recovered, her eyes met the stunned eyes of Arjen.

"I should not have brought you here," raved Dendros. "But I wanted you to at least feel the beauty of it before I killed you. Is all not as I had promised—peace, greenness, immortality—for seeds are immortal. When their seed-sacs grow full, the roof will be opened and the wind will take the shining seed-dust and spread it abroad, thus ensuring other Gardeners, other Gardens."

As he spoke, Arjen was slowly advancing on the vats, as if he could not bear to be near them. With the hilt of his sword, he struck at the glass and a crack appeared.

"Do not threaten my Seedlings."

Scorpia covered him with her sword. "Break them all, Arjen."

"I, as you see me, am not the true Gardener—when I played as a boy among these ruins, I found some shining dust in a casket and breathed it in. He is the true Seed, and *He* is terrible."

Arjen struck again and an opening appeared through which water began to gurgle.

Dendros stood smiling for a moment, his skin seeming greenly translucent. The tip of a bud appeared at one edge of his eye, squeezing back the eyeball in its outward progress. Similar buds, followed by green vines, surged from his nostrils, poked from his mouth like a green tongue. Fronds unfurled and waved and thorns began to protrude along the vine's length, a dark liquid forming on their tips.

Motionless for the moment in the horror of it, Scorpia saw a coil of vines tighten on Arjen's legs. She jerked back as a spiraling creeper reached for her wrist. Arjen held his sword two-handed and hacked at the vine's length, but its toughness blunted his sword. A tangle of growth crawled toward Scorpia, dragging along the husk-like body of Dendros in a way that made her feel sick. She began striking at the vines as they enveloped her legs, the thorns digging into the flesh. The blue sword did not grow blunt, but she saw her blows become weaker and felt the thorns pouring a substance into her body to make it heavy, yearning toward sleep. She saw Arjen drop. The whole room seemed filled with the awful vine.

"All this from one Seed," she said to herself dully. And began to struggle against the enveloping tendrils, toward the body of Dendros. With her arms gripped by the thorns, she had to tear her own flesh to get free enough for one, solid strike, cleaving the brittle skull of Dendros to expose the spore that had eaten his brain. The seed had a milky, translucent surface and from it branched the terrible creepers. Her sword-hilt smashed down on it once, twice, and the spore exploded into milky fragments. The complex of vine spasmed once and relaxed. Though it didn't matter, she worked her way free of the thorny tangle before lying down to the sleep the thorns had induced. She slipped into that blackness, not even knowing what kind of sleep it was.

Arjen awoke her, and she smiled up at his homely, weathered face, glad that she had awakened at all. "We must soon be away from this place," he said. "It's an abomination."

She sat up, examining the puncture wounds along her arms and legs. For a moment she was still half-drugged and could not understand the look of pain and horror still on Arjen's face, so she taunted him a little. "Old grudges are forgotten then; I need not reach for my sword."

He spoke gruffly, thrusting her sword into her hands. "Dendros has left us a fell harvest. We will need each other's human comfort and courage to do what we must." Understanding at last, she looked toward the vats where the children moved like lazy swimmers in their green dreams.

A Witch In Time

The guts of the city, the labyrinthian network of side streets and half forgotten alleyways, stirred with life even as the dayside city slept. An aged whore leaned out of a doorway where the smell of piss hung strongly in the air, her shapeless mouth drawn up into a withered grin as if someone had tightened the string of a well worn leather pouch.

"By Xesis, that'd take the lust out of a man, just the sight of her, let alone the smell."

His companion let the remark pass, as he often did when he was following his own oblique thoughts. "Don't let anyone come too close by you here. Babes in their mothers' arms are weaned on purse-snatching."

A lone man shouldered by them in the narrow alley where dampness beaded the stones. His face in the dull green glow of moonlight was crossed with a wide silvery scar that led into an eye that was only an empty sac of puckered flesh.

Wyle shuddered. "In this place they play rough. I hope we can soon find the one the old toad wants."

"We will. I've seen her often hereabouts, prowling the streets or running with a pack."

They continued their progress between moldering buildings that jostled each other for space. Balconies jutted out over the street from which the house slops might conveniently be emptied. They passed the inert body of a man, who was either drunk or dead (in this place it hardly mattered). Alek said something under his breath and pushed Wyle into the side of a building. A circle of small figures was gathered in the street, grotesque with bony elbows and knees in awkward positions and ragged garments flapping around their bodies. They seemed to playing a game as they shrieked and pounded each other. Alek motioned him forward, and Wyle saw, as they drew closer, a band of street urchins, gambling and squabbling over a small pile of treasure that must have been loot. A scrawny girl, with uncut shag of hair that turned blue/black/violet as she moved in the dim light, squealed as the die fell and with a quick gesture snatched up a golden bracelet and an empty silk purse.

"That one," directed Alek and the two men ran forward. The children took to their heels, disappearing into alleys, doorways, the foul-smelling shadows themselves. Wyle saw the girl slip into an almost hidden side street, half blocked by a fallen and decayed house.

"Haste. She moves through this dung heap like a swallow through air."

They explored the turnings of the narrow way but could not find where she had gone.

"There," said Alek and he was pointing to the ground where lay a circle of gold. "All we need to do is bide in the shadows awhile." Alek's narrow face radiated a tense happiness.

Wyle wasn't so sure his partner was right, and his muscles were beginning to complain of his cramped posture beneath a broken stairway when a small noise alerted him. Bending low to the ground and constantly turning her head as she looked and listened acutely, the girl searched for the bracelet. Her hand was just closing over the golden circle when Wyle, sneaking up behind her, grabbed her arm. "I've been stabbed!" he roared as something tore at his face. The flesh in his grasp was electric; it writhed, twisted . . . something like a trap closed on his fingers. By this time he had let go, but Alek had both hands on the girl's throat and was squeezing.

"Alek, let go," said Wyle without much conviction as he nursed his lacerated hand. "The frog-face wants something more than a corpse, I'll wager. We'll not collect our wages this way."

"'Tis said this Arcana is a witch and I don't want her putting any of her spells on me."

"'Tis said by washerwomen and puling old men," laughed Wyle. "Come now, Man, she's turning blue."

Arcana felt the world returning by slow stages. Only it was up-side down. Her throat was constricted with bright bands of pain and below her head two boot heels rang on the paving stones. She was being carried like a sack and was very uncomfortable but she decided it might be best to feign unconsciousness, then surprise them when her feet touched the ground. *If only I hadn't come back for the bracelet.*

The city began to take on a new aspect: streets widened, dwell-ings became newer and well-cared for, built with space between them. *What a waste,* thought Arcana. *There are no hiding places. Where can the people of this sector hide when the guards are after them?*

She felt herself carried through a door and closed her eyes as she was lowered to a smooth, cold floor. She would count ten slowly, open her eyes for a look, then run. Her eyes opened as she was scrambling to her feet, but a quick look showed her that she was alone in the room. There were two doors, both locked and a win-dow, too high and narrow.

The room she found herself in was huge with a vaulted ceiling and a floor of dark wood polished to mirror surface. The tapestries that softened the walls were woven in vibrant colors in the images of huntsmen, stags, warriors, maidens, and unicorns that moved as if with life when the draft along the cold walls stirred them subtly. The furniture intimidated her; delicate chairs of exotic wood hand rubbed until they glowed like jewels forbade even the thought that anyone might sit in them, especially Arcana in her ragged black shirt and trousers, smelling richly of life on the street.

A tray of food was on one of the tables and after sniffing it to see if she could detect poison, she ate, tearing meat off the bones and stuffing her mouth with fresh fruit as if someone was waiting to snatch it away. She was wiping the grease from around her mouth with a ragged sleeve when the door opened. Two panting servants staggered into the room, their arms extended to form a chair, and between them they carried something . . . a man, his body grown gross with age and gluttony. His neckless head sprouted from the collar of a burgundy robe as though someone had dressed a frog in velvet. Brown spots mottled his fragile skin and his eyes swam in rheum.

With a grunt of relief, the servants deposited this mound of sentient garbage in a love seat of emerald brocade. A smaller chair would have been crushed under that weight.

"My little dear, come closer. So that I may see you. My old eyes . . ." Out of the girl's mouth came easily a spate of obscenities (on close summer nights she had often sat below the balconies of the local whorehouse where the girls had appeared in the dusk like pale, parasitic flowers). Wyle and Alek had entered silently to stand behind Arcana but only Wyle laughed.

"Bring the witchlet closer. So that I may see her."

She was shoved almost into the soft bulk of the old man's belly. "Yesss, Arcana, Guardian of the Violet Door." His breath was the slime on the surface of stagnant ponds and his voice resonated through the layers of fat like music in some obscene instrument.

"I've heard of such a door," said Arcana, a guileless look appearing all too naturally upon her young face. "And many another such tale as old women tell in their idle moments."

The old man called a servant who brought him a garnetwood chest, carved in a disquieting pattern of flowers, fruit and snakes. "Here. Look at this," he said opening the box and thrusting it forward in his shaking hands.

Wyle pushed her forward again and she ground her teeth together as if wishing to bite yet not quite daring to. Then her gaze entered the chest and stayed there. Something was there, that was certain. But she couldn't make sense of it. A numbness grew behind her eyes and she jerked as if a cold hand had touched her. The fat man shut the box with a click, turning an ornate golden key. Arcana squeezed her eyes shut and shuddered. "What did you do? What have you taken from me?"

"How quickly you. Put your finger on it," said the old man and laughed so hard that he began to cough and wheeze, the phlegm in his throat rattling nastily. "You shall have it back. When you return.

If you have done well, Sweeting. I have heard it told that the violet door opens. All ways—even into Time's Center.

"You say nothing," he continued. "I see you know the place. Only someone like me. Could appreciate the gifts. That such a land can bestow—eternal youth. And happiness. It is for this. That you will bargain. With the Time lords."

"The rulers of Time, I can't—"

"Oh but you must do it. For me, my Pretty." His thumb and forefinger pinched Arcana's cheek with more than playfulness. She looked at the carven box and felt mortality slip down around her like a cumbersome garment.

"And you, Alek, and you, Wyle. Will go with her. Do not let her fail. With eternal youth and happiness. I will not need my house. My treasures. They will. Be yours."

Arcana led the way back through her maze of alleys. Inside the ruined shell of a stone building she entered a gap between two fallen pillars and scraped a pile of rubble off a wooden trap door. There was a straight drop of about seven feet and then a tunnel that slanted downward. A damp wind blew perpetually through the passageways and at times they were crawling on stomachs and elbows through incredibly narrow places and at others they passed through sticky webs that clung gauze-like to their faces (they only imagined the spiders).

"Here." Arcane tossed the word carelessly into dead silence, but they could see nothing.

Blindingly: a hairline crack of intense pink-violet. And then, seeing only the radiance with patterns overlaid by the weakness of their eyes, they went through the violet door. And shrill shrieks, a landscape of broken glass, bright & yellow & sizzling, smell and feel of wet fur—(all this and more) spun through their fragile and overloaded sensory equipment.

The sun (if it is the sun) stands still in Time's Center, giving off a clear and steady illumination. Arcana and her companions stand on a plain of white crystals, a field of warm, unmelting snow. As they move across this timescape, the smooth granules slip back into their footprints as if no one had ever passed this way. Arcana is remembering a face, immobile, as if abraded from stone. The expression of this face will be patient beyond belief.

"What do you see?" asks Wyle.

"Nothing. I was just trying to recall something. I don't think it was important."

They wander about disorientedly on the shining plain; Alek sees a tree and they make for it as the only landmark on a barren horizon. As they stand beneath the bare and crooked branches, a timewind causes buds to unfurl into fresh green leaves, and as suddenly shrivel, die and fall. Arcana remembers that she will walk down the leisurely paths of an artificial garden of some rigid material, made by a craftsman who had a passion for detail. "I know where to find them," says Arcana. "I remember it—no—I mean I'm remembering what will happen. Can't you?"

"Wait. A little," says Wyle, "but I can't—it's all ajumble."

"This place has addled your minds," says Alek, the barely suppressed look of fear on his acid face betraying him. "No one can remember the future."

"Perhaps not, but my memory has shown me the way to a Time Lord's castle." She strides out boldly, knowing that they will follow her, but though some of the future lies in her memory, it is fragmentary, imperfect, mixed in with a chaotic past. It becomes frightening to think of it, so she concentrates on walking.

The sun vanishes—a wind, blowing in all directions at once, tears at clothing, hair; tosses debris into their faces until in the darkness they call out and try to reach one another. Arcana stumbles against someone; she reaches out and clasps his hand. The flesh is solid to the touch, then melts like wax against her fingers, growing smaller, bonier. Crooked fingers clutch her hand. The wind screams.

When Arcana opens her eyes she is confronted by a stranger, an ancient man with sparse white hair and cheek and jawbone thrusting out against brown-paper skin.

"Alek!" shouts Wyle and "Alek?" as he begins to know the old man's face, the mouth twisting in the familiar bitter smile.

"Give my love to the fat frog," he says, "and use his money better than he knew how to."

Arcana holds the crooked hand of a corpse, and reluctantly she lets it go. "I would return now," says Wyle, "so that another old man can know what it is to die." He mutters the curses that serve him for tears.

"He was caught in a freak vortex of the timewind," says Arcana. "Nothing is as it should be here."

"You knew it would happen? Then why didn't you warn us?" He grips her by the wrists and shakes her.

"Knowing the past doesn't mean that you can change it. It's the same with the future." She suddenly finds it hard to look into his ugly, kind-natured face. He lets her go, shakes his head over Alek's body.

Arcana knows the way now and something of what lies before. They need stop for neither food nor water, for as long as they are here, the cells of their bodies are unchanging. Arcana feels herself playing a kind of game that she truly doesn't care about. She thinks of the wine-red chest and wonders what can be in it to make her feel that nothing matters, that even the sadness she feels now is too unimportant for tears.

A gray structure appears before them, tall, cylindrical, reminiscent of a castle in its color and conformity (though it is perhaps something else entirely). Arcana and Wyle arrive at a seamless gray wall with great metal gates. At first the wall looks too smooth for climbing, but Arcana's eye, trained in burglary, sees some depressions and projections on the stone, and monkeywise she swarms up the wall, leaving Wyle gaping below her.

Dropping lithely down inside, she tugs at the heavy bar on the gate, but to her strength, at least, it is immovable. "You'll have to wait for me," she shouts to Wyle, unseen.

She takes the path toward the castle, noticing the grass and flowers that border the path. Though the lawn is brilliant green, it is rigid beneath her fingers as she bends to touch it. And though the flowers are of radiant colors and have a look of freshness, they too, seem artificial. All else is the same; the willows whose foliage arches and trails fluidly to the ground, even the very insects of the place. Beneath the willows she sees two figures and she walks toward them, not sure she wants to make contact with the Lords of Time,

She pauses, seeing that the two are but statues, though beautifully and realistically made. One is a lady, dressed in a white gown that hangs in elegant folds from a voluptuous body. The other statue is seated and the face is so familiar, so patient, so pleasing with its full beard and lines around the eyes that she wishes to climb up into his lap and lean her face against his. At last she does so and stays there for some moments, thinking that the body of the statue is giving back some answering warmth. She can feel its pulse, but she soon realizes that it is her own blood beat transferred to unliving stone. Feeling foolish and wiping wetness out of her eyes, she climbs down. This is not getting her where she needs to go. As she approaches the gray castle, it buries her in its shadow; she feels the weight of that shadow as if centuries have passed as she nears the tall brass doors. She shivered, feeling herself standing at the door of a tomb—she knows that there is nothing alive here. A large wrought iron bell hangs beside the door, and she pulled the cord; the bell moves imperceptibly, but there will be no sound. The doors are tight against her, but trailing streamers of stone ivy decorate the walls and these allow her to climb up to one of the narrow windows. It will be easy to wiggle her scrawny body through and drop (landing on her feet) on the tessellated floor. The room was. She cannot describe it in any way except that it is like lying back and looking up at the cold perfection of the stars until a feeling of helpless fear makes you quickly look away. She went from room to room, afraid to call out, and even more afraid of meeting whatever lived in this austere environment. No one or no thing is here, and she must wait until it decides to return.

"There is a ghost in the house."

Idrene picks a starflower from a bush where blossoms have opened in cream-white profusion all the long summer. She laughs and turns to face her husband, tucking the flower into the red richness of her hair.

"I have felt it passing through the garden just now. I think it touched me." (A generation was born and died as he spoke.)

"You were dreaming"—(Mountains weathered; rivers cut new channels through porous earth.)—"as you dozed in your chair."

"No, it flew through the garden like a moth; I almost saw it."

Arcana wandered a dim passageway; the atmosphere of the place hangs heavy on her shoulders, squeezed about her rib cage. Emerging into yet another room, she sees the red haired statue that she has come to accept as a motif, a constantly recurring part of the decor. This room contorted itself wildly with mirrors set at crazy angles. Everything in the room was reflected endlessly, but when she looks for herself, her own reflection is missing. She touched her narrow face, outlined her sharp nose and felt the softness of her eyes under their lids. When she was able to verify her existence, she began to snoop about the room. An enameled jewel box was set back on a shelf in one of the cleverly concealed closets. In it she finds a necklace of jewels that did not glitter but burned with a steady interior light. She clasps it around her neck where it glowed against the greasy fibers of her old shirt. She will explore the rest of the gigantic house at her leisure, feeling not the absence of time, but its absolute presence.

"I heard the bell ring this morning," he said, "and when I answered it"—(In a real world, war was fought and two treaties were written and broken.)—"no one was there."

"You'd have me seeing ghosts in every dark corner." Her laugh was deep and thick, resonating up from her ample chest cavity. (Great trees grew to immense size in a land where no one saw them.) Arcana kept busy by accumulating treasures—too many, she knows, to take them all with her, but she only does it to avoid remembering too much. She had recalled a richly-appointed, though familiar, room. She had felt so cold and brittle, the very sound of the wind outside the high windows was threatening. When she had looked down at herself she had seen the fallen breasts of an old woman, the dried-leaf hands. It should have been a reassuring memory, but it isn't.

"My necklace has been stolen!" She was vibrant with rage. (A species of flightless birds dwindled in number, became extinct.)

"Now you see the handiwork of my ghost."

"You don't really think—"

"I think I must manage to contact this ghost. It haunts us for a purpose of its own."

"You would catch a thing of air and an overcrowded imagination?"

"If I want to."

Arcana will enter the library, an echoing place webbed thick with shadows. The rows of books along the walls reminded her of tombstones, each with its neat inscription. She made a quick intake of breath as she turned and saw the statue. It is standing in front of a row of books as if studying the titles. "I don't remember seeing you in here before, but you look like you belong in this room." She spoke to him in the usual, slightly impertinent tone; she always found herself talking to this particular statue. She had thought it funny at first, but she didn't feel like laughing now. Her body is beginning to feel an immense sluggishness. She would have dropped into a chair from the weight of her own body, but her legs have become rigid. Then her perceptions went crazy as the statue moved—the eyes blinked.

"You see, Idrene. I have our ghost."

The female statue, now animate, crossed the room to stare angrily at Arcana. "My necklace!" She tears it from Arcana's throat, breaking the clasp.

"You're from the real world," said the Time Lord with a certain awe.

"I am Arcana, Witch of the Crossways," she says, hearing the incredible slow, low tones of her own voice. "1 have come to bargain with you on behalf of the Duke of Glain."

"You would bargain with"—he laughed sharply—"a Lord of Time for this, this ephemeral heap of ordure who calls himself powerful. In your world I could walk out and gather children like you as one would pick bouquets of wildflowers, and before midday all would be withered and dying in my hands." In his laughter was all the careless cruelty of time. "So, my light fingered ghost, you've managed to slide into Time's Center and into my stronghold. Let's bargain in earnest and I'll set you a quest. If you win it, you may make your Lord's request. You must enter the forest where leaves fall forever: and find a certain dwelling. I think you will know it when you see it; most worldlings do. A mysterious hermit you will find there wears a ring like none you have ever seen. Bring it to me."

"As good as done," says Arcana, turning to go.

"There is one warning I must give you. Do not look directly upon his face."

Arcana felt herself growing lighter as he speaks. The lips of the statue are hardening, the eyes glazing. Arcana stretched her arms and legs, feeling as if she is awakening from a too long, too deep sleep. Yet she knows she has not been dreaming because the Time Lady held the recovered necklace around her plump white throat. Immediately Arcana feels that she wants to be away from this place. There was an alien aspect to the Time Lord's face that has not been apparent to her until now. Centuries will pass like the slow grinding of stone on stone before that carven smile, those dead eyes, would change.

She began to run, down an indigo corridor, mad with deep-water reflections, up to a window and through it into the light of an eternally ascendant sun. The weight and dust-smell of centuries fall away as she scales the wall, the stone abrading her hands and knees.

"Wyle!" She half-fell from the wall and ran forward to assail him.

"I didn't know if you'd come out of there or not," Wyle says, when he is able to make sense of her jabbering. "But waiting isn't hard here. One minute is much the same as the next. I was dreaming, or maybe I wasn't even asleep. I walked through a place of shadows and a long figure without a face—"

"Forget your dreams. The Time Lord has given us a quest. If we fulfill it, he will grant the Duke's request. We'll be able to leave this awful place. Come, I'll tell you, as we walk, what the Lords of Time are like and how they live."

A duskiness in the air and shadows had begun to envelop them. They had sensed rather than seen the trees about them, ancient and twisted trees, whose upper branches were obscured in distance and blurred by the intense blueness of the air. The utter silence of the place had intimidated them, but Arcana had reached out to take Wyle's hand. Leaves like pale silver outlines of ghosts were whispering down from above, slowmotion falling, drifting, twisting, hypnotic in their motion. Arcana had felt that she was being buried alive in the light crispness of leaves and their warm organic smells and she wished she could die with them, grow brown and withered and gone.

Only a terrible inner toughness that life on the street had given her kept her on her feet. Wyle tries to lie down, but she kicks him sharply. They wade knee deep in the curling crisp leaves, drunk on the smell of leaf-mold, half in love with the perpetual dying season of the year.

"There," says Wyle.

A dimness is all they can see, a gathering mass of solid shadow. "You said it would be easy, but I don't like this place. I've been here before, or to someplace like it." Wyle nervously caresses the smooth staghorn handle of his dagger.

"It's only a house—looks kind of deserted, though. I didn't think you'd be afraid of haunts or spirits." She walks forward boldly, too young to feel what Wyle feels about the place. The stones hang together precariously, furred with green-black moss. Wings rustle in the branches above, but Arcana sees no birds. The door stands open.

At first Wyle will not enter; his knuckles are white as he grips his weapon. Arcana has to laugh at him, careless, cruel child's laughter that rings (somehow) familiar in her ears. And he follows into the cave-damp interior of the deserted house. The room is barren; a rough bed tied with thongs and heaped with dried evergreen boughs, a huge gnarled tree-stump hollowed out into a chair, polished dark and smooth by the body of someone who had often sat there, staring into a fire on the raw-brick hearth, seeing Xesis knew what visions. Arcana tries to shake off the feeling of uneasiness that is creeping up the back of her neck. Footsteps crackle in the leaves outside, paralyzing Wyle with fear. Arcana guides him to a corner where a heavy crossbeam casts down a bar of darkness. Someone enters, ducking to avoid hitting his head on the door. As he passes Arcana averts her eyes, remembering the Time Lord's warning, but she cannot help looking once he was gone by. He is gangling, raw-boned, but does not move in a clumsy way. His ragged shirt exposes long wristbones, strangely delicate to end in large, ungainly hands which are darkly stained. His coarse black hair curls down over his collar. Arcana finds herself wishing that he will turn around.

He picks up a log and drops it into the fireplace. The dry wood seems to blaze up almost as he touches it. He sits down on the chair and extends his hands, letting the firelight turn them redly translucent. He seems a lonely figure, trying to bring warmth to this lost place. Arcana impulsively wishes to stand beside him, dispelling the long loneliness with a word and spend the eternal evening in talk or companionable silence. As the figure relaxes, seems to fall into a light sleep, his hand drops, almost to the floor, firelight sparking off the frost-silver of a large ring.

Arcana is immediately all hard business as her eyes catch that spark. "I'll sneak up close and if he's asleep, I'll slip the ring from his finger."

Wyle gripped`her convulsively. "No, you mustn't touch him. The Time Lord played us false. I think I know this man. Only he isn't properly a man."

"Quiet, he'll waken." Wyle's eyes slip nervously sideways, to see if what she says is happening.

"And even he sleeps," he says, letting his hands slip weakly from Arcana's shoulders.

Her taut muscles carry her across the room, her bare feet making only the softest of sounds. But the sleeper breathes deeply, regularly, even when her fingers delicately grip the ring. It is ice, sending a shudder through her. Where the set should be is a dark opening like a tiny well that is so deep she has to keep herself from looking into it for too long. She thinks there are certain things stirring at the bottom of the well. It isn't difficult for her to slide the ring off the lax finger. She clasps the treasure against her palm, motioning Wyle toward the door. His foot makes a scraping sound and the creature before the fire is thrusting himself upward. Though Arcana does not look back, in her peripheral sight he seems to tower upward, growing to an impossible height. She lets her fear propel her to necessary speed as she bolts through the door. Looking back over her shoulder, she sees Wyle, running slowly like a figure trapped in a dream, and unbelievably, turning his head, turning to look back at the face of what pursues him; it is just as she remembers it.

Wyle's legs let his body fall of its own weight and he settled to the ground, all knowledge all pain all fear all joy sliding from his features glazing over into a terrible peace. And so final. So she could see nothing but the blurred prisms of her own tears and something was tearing its way out of her, but she could still run, so, of course she did.

And, of course, she got away, with the ring a burning cold circle in her hand and with a gnawing curiosity that made her wish that she, too, had looked back. It would have been one way of solving the mystery.

The Time Lord's statue stands in the indigo passageway, looking out a window as if it were waiting for her return. She will fling the silver ring at his feet. "The quest is done, you stupid, smug, stone bastard."

Seablue light danced across her eyes and she felt herself grow ponderous again. The statue moved, stooped, picks up the ring, seemingly unoffended, yet perhaps her ghost-words had never reached his ears. He appears strangely pleased and reaches out to draw her nearer, but she shrugged off his touch. "I want nothing of you for myself, but my master wishes eternal youth and happiness, little may it profit the ill-smelling old crocodile."

The Time Lord looks at her in surprise (as though a flower from his lovely bouquet had calmly spit in his eye).

A servant poured wine from the cobwebbed bottle into the crystal goblet and put it carefully into the frail, brown spotted hand. "It's cold in here," whined the old lady. The stags and hounds and maidens and unicorns moved with constant life along the walls. "The wind is rising again; I can hear it."

"Yes, Ma'am, but it's only the wind after all," answered the servant, a surreptitious smile appearing on his youthful face.

"Yes." Her querulous voice subsided and she looked around the room. It had changed very little. The small jewel-polished chairs and tables stand superciliously in their places, mirrored in the shining floor.

Another servant appeared at the door. "My Lady, the little gentlemen is ready for bed." A child rushed into the room, a bloom of red curls, a bird-egg speckling of freckles. "Good night, my angel," said the old lady. A line of spittle drooled down the boy's chin from his open mouth; his eyes shone with a heavenly, a mindless happiness. He made squealing sounds and grabbed at invisible butterflies as the maidservant led him from the room. "Good night, my little duke. Such a good boy, such a *happy* boy." She nearly strangled on her own high, witch-laughter.

The night wind prowled endlessly, sending unseen filaments to pluck at the tapestries and make the fire flutter on the hearth. The old lady's head nodded forward, like a heavy pod on a slender stem. Dry leaves zig-zagged leisurely to the ground.

"I've lost my way," shouted Arcana, her voice deadened in this quiet place.

"Follow me," said a voice and Alek appeared beside her. She followed him among dark trees, but his strides were long and she had to run to keep up.

"You're going in circles," she accused him at last, grabbing hold of his sleeve. He started laughing and grasping firmly the skin of his forehead, he began to peel it off easily, exposing the face of Wyle. It was peaceful, as she had last remembered it. Without speaking he gently led her along a path bordered with stone willows and starflower shrubs. She picked a flower and felt it cool and rigid against her cheek. Wyle smiled and seated himself in one of the garden chairs. She knew what was coming but still she felt her stomach contract when he removed the membraneous mask and became the Time Lord.

"*You* are Arcana?" he asked. "You are much changed. I only dozed off for a moment . . ."

"Years have passed and with them, my life, a life crowded with things happening, people coming and going. But you have not changed at all." She placed the starflower in his open hand.

He rose, holding the flower before him, where it began to flame and sizzle and throw sparks, illuminating a great darkness ahead. She walked close beside his lanky, scarecrow figure, content, for in a moment he would peel back the final mask and she would see his face.

DEMON AND DEMOISELLE

Arcana pulled rein on a wooded mountainside and lifted her arm where the nervous falcon swayed heavily, clasping and unclasping his talons to steady his uncertain perch. His back and wing feathers were the sad color between blue and gray; his chest and legs were shadowbarred. She contemplated the vasty reach of sky for some moments and at last saw a pigeon flying. She hastily removed the black leather hood and the jesses and sent the falcon upward with an arm thrust and a cry. He climbed as if there were no such thing as gravity, and overtaking the pigeon in his speed, wheeled above it, windwalking. Just as he would have stooped to take the helpless bird in his talons, the falcon's body jerked, a few feathers drifting away on the wind. The great wings parachuted the fall, but to Arcana on the ground it took an inordinately long time for the body to fall to earth. She ran to where it lay among some trees and knelt beside the mound of rumpled feathers. Folly to think that one could be attached to a thing as stupid and rapacious as a bird of prey, but the beauty of its flight, the lofty power of it—The bird was transfixed by an arrow of ivory with peacock feathers on the end of the shaft; it looked like a decorative piece, not a weapon. She ran back into the open, to search for a bowman or fleeing horseman, but nothing moved on the mountainside. A dark wisp of hair by her ear moved, and she started, but decided that it was a gust of wind that had frightened her. Her huge black horse was pawing the earth, the feathers of his forelegs shaking like fine black fringe. "Sooo, Sable," she soothed him. "We're both spooked by nothing. Or we can hope it's nothing." Sable's basin-sized hooves rattled the drawbridge and struck fire from the cobbles of the courtyard. She felt better when the creaking machinery had lifted the bridge into a massive wall behind her. She left the horse to the grooms and entered the castle. She doubled herself as she entered, reflecting darkly in the polished wood of the floor. Everything seemed good, the blood red hangings on the walls, the great hearth blazing like HellMouth, throwing off the chill of such a large drafty room. Her Seneschal Milston came in to personally divest her of cloak and gauntlets.

"I watched you ride in just now as if someone pursued. And where is your favorite, Windrider?"

Stony visaged, Arcana dropped into a straightbacked chair as large as a throne and every bit as uncomfortable. "He was shot by—" her explanation halted while she rummaged for mislaid reasons. "Some poacher hiding in the brush of the mountainside," she finished lamely.

Milston said nothing. and drew his face into careful lines of politeness, telling her that for all the world, he wouldn't pry.

"His wounds. Milston, of course it wasn't just any ordinary poacher or huntsman. The arrow came from nowhere; I misdoubt me it was shot from a bow at all. And it isn't just that; a kind of dread haunts my bones like an ague. I must to the tower." The tower, in contrast to the chambers below, was a cold and barren place. Spiders had left samples of their craft in niches of the bare rock walls and rats' droppings collected in the concave risers of the stone stairway. She produced a huge iron key from inside her clothing, opened the massive lock and let herself into the single round room where she practiced her craft. Yellowing scrolls and books with moldering, flaking bindings were shelved along the walls. Bottles and jars filled with questionable substances of every color and texture filled the interstices between the books. On a rickety wooden table an iron-bound book lay open to reveal slanting lines of spidery black handwriting and a scrying glass half filled with water. Alongside these was a toad, looking very dry and petrified. Set in his back among the warty excrescences of his skin was a red jewel, filled with fiery light. When she moved the book the ancient toad hopped off silently, toadwise.

With a bit of charcoal she drew the pentagram on the stones of the floor, recoloring a faded design that had often been drawn there. Lighting five candles, she placed them at the corners of the

pentagram and began the ritual, referring now and again to the
open book on the table. Sometime later she dropped onto a bench,
pushing dark strands of hair off her damp forehead. Stolidly she rose
to try again. because she had never failed at this before. Moments
later the scrying glass and the book went flying off the table, one to
splash and shatter on the stones, the other to fetch up against the
wall, a broken black wing. "God's Little Body!" she swore.
"Hrinegar, do you know aught of this?"

A small melancholic voice came from the floor and the aged
toad hopped in its silkily silent progression, pausing at the sorceress'
feet. "Mayhap your demon has been ensorceled by another mage."

"But that demon was the only one I could summon. It took
years of study and experimentation to produce him. Without him, I
can't even call myself sorceress. Who did it; do you know?"

"No, but if you hadn't acted in such haste, you may have scryed
something on the matter."

"I'm too choleric to concentrate on that now."

"Then perhaps you don't care to know." She gritted her teeth
for a moment, then found another glass goblet and poured some
water into it. Scrying consisted mainly of hours of staring and wasn't
among Arcana's favorite activities. but she bent dutifully over the
glass, and when she felt that her eyes were frozen in their sockets, an
image began to form in the midst of clear water.

"I see," she said in a carefully controlled voice, so as to maintain
her concentration.

"What do you see?" asked the toad peevishly (though everything he said sounded peevish).

"A face, old, more than old, seamed and eroded, hanks of greasy
gray hair hanging about a bald pate, a nose long and drooping as an
icicle. but his eyes—"

"Yes?"

"His eyes make it seem as if he is wearing a mask. They glow
with the hot-bloodedness of youth, yet they also seem to be looking
out of some other, unwholesome world." Her voice grew more excited. "In his hands he holds an ivory arrow. He's our man, but who

is he?"

"I should not tell you," said the toad in a voice more dismal (if that were possible) than heretofore.

"Why not? He has my demon and I want him back."

"That's why I dare not tell you, a neophyte, a beginner, a rank—"

"Of course you'll tell me Hrinegar, old familiar." She stooped to grab him and he punished her toadfashion by wetting copiously.

She made a disgusted noise and dried her hands on the legs of her hunting costume. "But you will tell me." She grabbed him more carefully this time, and his skinny old legs thrashed comically.

"Ascarius, you fool. Ascarius. He has been an archimage longer than you have been a human, longer than I have been a toad, longer than the oak-giant in the forest has been a tree. He has read all the old books. He has written some of them before reading them. He commands seven demons!"

"Eight." she said, putting Hrinegar carefully onto the floor where he loped silently away, his stone spitting sparks. "That co-ney-catcher has preyed off his fellow mages for the last time. I'll to his keep and teach the old dodderer a lesson."

Arcana paused before the drawbridge, the massive head of the shire, Sable, poised above her shoulder as she pulled on her gauntlets. Though she had looked slim and feminine in the close-fitting hunting garb, with her long hair plaited, she now looked bulky in a leather vest and thick broidered cloak, and beneath the flat cap her hair hung in bluntly cut tufts. Mil had suggested if she had to go, she go in the guise of a wandering scop. He had even found a battered old lute and hung it over her shoulder. He had done a good job disguising her, but still he hemmed and hawed and invented excuses to detain her.

"I'm pleased to know you fear for me," said Arcana, "but there's no need. Do you doubt my horsemanship?"

"Of course not, my Lady."

"Then what is it?"

"Your cooking, my Lady. Take no offense, but I am afraid you may fall ill. Have you taken sufficient provisions?"

Arcana swung up and signaled the man on the parapet. "I'll worry about you, too," she said. "If the villagers below realize that I'm devoid of power, they'll arrange a torchlight procession and come up to tear apart my keep, stone by stone."

"We'll keep up appearances as long as possible. God speed."

"Fare thee well, Milston."

Many and many the miles Arcana rode in rain and sun. And too diverse and blood-chilling were her adventures, up hill and down dale, to tell the whole of them, but after her travels had left her seasoned and wizened, she came to an inn to pass the night.

As she prepared to enter she heard a terrible din. She side-stepped a human projectile that careened out the door. Waiting until the noise had subsided, she entered cautiously, her hand on the hilt of her dagger. A ruffian was curled in a corner in a posture too awkward for sleep. Another lay beneath a table, his jerkin soaked with blood; luckily most of it was streaming from his nose. She flattened herself against the wall as a mace was slammed onto a heavy oaken table with a rending crash. The man in armor dominated the room like a monster of metal, but he clattered and clanged as he swayed unsteadily.

A man hiding beneath a table waved her away. "He's taken leave of his senses. Too much strong drink."

The man in armor began to growl deep in his throat as he yanked at the mace, now inextricably one with the wood of the table. "For the Holy Rood!" he bellowed. "Onward to the grail." Arcana began to move crabwise along the wall, but any movement was a mistake. The knight bore down on her like a juggernaut. "Avaunt pagan dog!"

The grid of a visor was thrust into her face, and a tang of ale was wafted toward her. "Who be you, stranger?"

"Arcan, a scop, teller of thrilling tales of bold knights and—" She thrust the lute between herself and him. His metal glove plucked the strings with a discordant sound.

"By Saint Allidore, I'll hear some of your drivel, and it had best be good."

Since in her travels she had neglected to learn to play the instrument she banged the strings once or twice and began to sing-song a tale that she devised on the spot. It was mostly utter nonsense about a faithful knight and his lady who sickened and died.

"Oh, my heart is broken. Oh my heart is sore. Verily, verily, now I shall die," she finished, giving the lute a strum for good measure. Having been caught up in her own creation, she looked up to see how the crazed knight was taking it.

"Oh my heart is sore," echoed the knight. "That's the saddest, most beautiful tale that ever I heard." He slumped onto a bench with a clang, his visored head resting in a pool of ale, his shoulders heaving.

"Thanks, stranger," said the hiding man, coming up to clap her on the shoulder.

"Verily," chimed in another who had been crouched by the hearth. "He'll be all right now. Simply boyish high spirits."

"Spirits of some type. Are any of you the innkeeper? I wish lodging for the night."

The knight lifted his head from the table and removed his helmet, displaying a pair of bleary blue eyes in a smiling red-bearded face. "You can share my room this night," he said,"for you cooled my madness with your song, and I fain would hear more of your tales."

"I must needs refuse this gentle offer." What seemed a half ton of metal descended on her shoulders and she was dragged down an ill-smelling corridor and deposited half crushed in a dimly lit room.

The knight began noisily to remove his armor. "Help me, man, my squire is one who lies in the tavern bleeding."

Arcana unbuckled the greaves from his shins while he divested himself of the rest, tossing it into a dully gleaming pile on the floor.

"Make yourself comfortable, Sirrah. The bed's got plenty of room. I told the landlord if there're lice in it, I'll spit him like a capon."

"I'm comfortable as I am." Arcana lay back on the rustling straw mattress and watched as the knight set up a tiny shrine and knelt before it. A few moments later the bed creaked in extremis and the knight shouldered her aside. She was uncomfortable, but not too afraid, as he didn't seem the type to molest boys.

"A knight must never forget his spiritual duties. My name is Ethelred of Ironcastle, but they call me Quickspur."

"Well met," said Arcana.

"Where are you bound, balladeer?"

"Where the wind takes me."

"By Allidore's sainted relics, why not accompany me on my travels? You're a singer in search of songs, so why not celebrate me?"

"Why not indeed." Arcana felt laughter overcoming her. Would he spit her like a capon if he heard her laugh?

"There are sure to be adventures amany because my quest takes me to the keep of a terrible magician, Ascarius. He holds captive the loveliest of maidens, Ermintrude, daughter of Lord Tabor. If I can rescue her, I shall receive her hand in marriage, though I know I am unworthy to touch the hem of her gown. A knight must adore his lady chastely, from afar."

Arcana had stopped shaking with laughter. "I'd be honored to accompany you, and to compose a saga at least of your victory over Ascarius." *And my own,* she added silently.

"Dragonslond," said Quickspur, gesturing toward a landscape of rocks and broken hills and stingy vegetation. The very trees were wind-twisted and ugly as if the land itself were cursed. Arcana saw a goat-footed unicorn atop a shaft of stone, but when she tried to point it out, it was gone. They passed a massive circle of standing stones and had an argument over it, Quickspur asserting that it had been raised by giants in the youth of the world, Arcana theorizing that such heavy stones could only be magicked into place; she suggested the magic of sound.

"Maybe they were whistled into place," said Quickspur, laughing at her.

"Hsst. I hear something. It sounds like the clink of mail—perhaps we are pursued by robbers."

"If so. it'll be the last time they molest honest men."

"No, look!"

It continued its slow majestic progress across their field of vision, its taloned feet splaying under its great weight, the scales of its sides chinking and clinking as it walked, its pointed tail drawing a wide straight track behind it. The sunlight shivered off the scales, dark green, black and bronze, here and there a glint of sapphire, a shimmer of ruby. Their horses began to dance and snort. The dragon turned his massive head in their direction, nictitating membranes flipping down over his lizard's eyes with chitinous click. A hiss issued from his maw and a dribble of smoke leaked out. A golden crest on head and shoulders began to rise.

"Let us flee," suggested Arcana. "Our horses are surely fleeter of foot than this weighty beast."

"Nonsense. Stand clear now."

"S'wounds, you're not going to—"

"Watch carefully. You'll want to chronicle this." Quickspur put spurs to his charger's sides and galloped toward the dragon, his lance at the ready. Arcana saw the dragon's corded belly flash icy-white as the thing reared up housetop high, towering over Quickspur and his tiny lance. Sparks began to shoot sideways from the jaws of the terrible worm, and as he huffed, a spurt of flame danced out, blasting the ground in front of Quickspur's horse's forefeet. The horse squalled and wheeled, Quickspur grabbing onto his neck. Somehow he managed to keep his seat and steer the crazed horse around to attack the dragon from the side but his lance broke against the glittering scales, and the impact sent him flying to the ground where he lay as helpless as an overturned lobster. Arcana screamed and reined Sable forward. As Quickspur lay there kicking his feet, the dragon went after his horse. It moved lizard-swift for all its bulk and landed on the fleeing animal with splayed forefeet, bearing it to the ground. The great jaws closed on the horse's head, flames licking from its clamped jaws and a terrible smell of burnt flesh filling the air. Arcana reached Quickspur and tried to lever him up. but he was too heavy, and the dragon was returning at an impossibly rapid trot. "Stay down," she called and began to run, racing in a zig-zag pattern as she kept in mind the jetting flames. She was not quite quick enough, however, because a stream of fire spurted between her elbow and ribs, charring her vest and setting her sleeve on fire. But she had reached her goal, a sloping ridge of loose rock, larger boulders looming toward the top. She scrambled up it, ignoring the bruises to her ankles and shins. For a moment she crouched there in the sliding talus and beat out the flames on her clothing, while the monster bellowed and shot a stream of flame that crackled just out of reach. Then she began to climb again, almost too hastily, for she fell full length and began to slide down. With an effort that left her trembling with exhaustion, she found firm purchase for her feet and climbed to the top where boulders perched on layers of loose rock.

She put her shoulder behind one and pushed. She felt something break and prayed it was nothing of hers. She toppled herself backward as the whole hillside tore loose and fell to meet the dragon just as he was valiantly trying to climb the shaly slope. When she peered over the ridgetop the rock was bearing him down, and then with a muted roar, covered him completely, a dust-haze obscuring the scene. For a moment she held her breath, thinking to see him digging out, but the largest stones must have done their work. When she returned to Quickspur, she noticed that the squire had taken to his heels. They were never to see him again.

Arcana righted Quickspur as best she could so that he could rise. He enfolded her in metallic embrace until she cried out because of her burns. "For a singer of idle tales you gave that dragon short shrift, but I didn't know if your plan would work. If those rocks hadn't fallen—"

"I whistled them down."

Toward evening the wind came up blowing rain, so they had to seek shelter in a cave. Arcana was afraid it might be a dragon's den, but Quickspur insisted, so being too tired to argue, she went inside. The entrance led through a narrow-walled tunnel so dark she had to feel her way along damp walls with her hands. In the darkness she suddenly felt herself grabbed and held; a hand grabbed her jaw, twisted her head around, then someone kissed her, full and forcefully on the lips, a tongue warm and wet forcing itself between her jaws. She was struggling when someone ran into her from behind, and suddenly she was fighting nothing.

"What's wrong? Did you hear another dragon?" Quickspur's voice matter-of-factly innocent.

Arcana stumbled forward. *Maybe he knows,* she thought, *or maybe I was wrong. Maybe he likes boys.* But when they reached a larger chamber of the cave, a dry and dragonfree place, Quickspur lay chastely beside her.

"I have heard that Ermintrude is truly lovely—a goddess. How dare that old lecher—My blood boils to think of it. I'll carry her from the castle and be her humble slave forever. By the bye, Arcan, if you compose a lay on our dragonslaying, I hope you, uh, don't mention—"

"I'll sing of your triumph over the worm so that generations will remember it," said Arcana, "but not now. I'm too sore, and too tired."

"I'll recompense you for this, friend," said Quickspur, and the arm about her shoulder was nothing but comradely.

Dragonslond dropped behind them, and they rode into a greener, more wholesome country. They rode up to the door of a country inn, looking like two scarecrows. The proprietor ushered them inside where there was steaming food served by red-cheeked peasant girls. "I knew I was missing something," said Quickspur, pinching a round bottom through voluminous homespun skirts. When Arcana gave him a scathing look he said confidingly, "There's something overdainty about you, lad. No offense, but it's time someone helped you to become more of a man."

"I'm as much man as I'll ever be, or need to be," said Arcana testily around a rare joint of meat that trickled bloody juices down her chin. "And what of your knightly vows of chivalry—chastity and reverence for womankind?"

Quickspur looked wounded. "I have all proper reverence for ladies, beautiful ladies, high-born ladies, but these are tavern wenches. List, while I give you a fatherly word on what to do with one of them." Quickspur leaned over and whispered in her ear while she listened with narrowed eyes, a corner of her mouth turning up ever so slightly, as if she didn't know whether to laugh or to sneer.

"Oh, they might scream bloody murder, but it's the right thing to do. It's what they want after all." He began to work on his joint of meat, his eyes still on the serving girls. Washed and wearing new clothes and lying back on a real bed, Arcana was feeling halfway human again and trying to plan a strategy that took into account Ascarius' power and Quickspur's impetuosity and her own cleverness, when the door began to vibrate as a booted foot was swung against it. "What can the dolt want now? If he wants to sleep in here I'll barricade the door. If he wants a song about his manly prowess with serving wenches I'll—Stop, you lout. You're splintering the door. Wait a moment and I'11 open—Bodikins! No!"

Quickspur had knocked on the door with his foot because he had a serving girl under each arm. Arcana tried to shut the door but he was already striding inside. "This one's for you." He dropped half his burden on the bed where she dissolved into giggles, hiding her red face with her hands. "Remember the instructions I gave you, yearling. I'll have you strutting out of here like a gamecock."

"But I don't—"

"Someone must take you in hand, lad." He went out, closing the door securely. She heard the sound of a heavy piece of furniture being dragged against it.

The girl on the bed was now peeking coyly from between her fingers.

"This is going to be very difficult to explain," said Arcana, perching daintily on the edge of the bed. When she saw the flirting expression on the girl's face, she knew that explanation of any kind was impossible, so she untied the thongs of her vest and pulled up her jerkin.

Now that the stunned serving girl was open to explanations, Arcana told her everything and gave her a silver coin for the tale she was to relate to Quickspur on the morrow. "I don't suppose you play cards," said Arcana producing a cunningly painted ivory deck from her waistband. "No? Well, I shall teach you—"

As they rode on their way the next day Arcana often found Quickspur looking at her surreptitiously. As they sat by their fire that night, he said, "That girl told me a story that curled my toes, but spill my spirit, if there's still not something girlified about you. The way the call of nature sends you skittering off behind rock or bush. Overnice, I call it. Mayhap—"

Arcana said no word, in protest nor explanation, but rolled up in her cloak beside the pink coals of their fire. Wolves reminded them that the night was dark and this country lonely, but not even fear could stave off sleep. She awoke from a dream in which someone was trying to ravish her. She had confused it somehow with the wolves' howls she had heard the evening before, and she fancied that sharp teeth had worried her neck and shoulders while blunt hands had touched and pawed at her breasts. She drew in her breath in a gasping half-scream and sat up. The thongs of her vest were untied, her jerkin rutched up as if her dream had come real. *No, I only struggled so in my dream to dislodge my clothing. Such a thing is nonsense* (or magic, insinuated a distant voice in her mind which she conveniently ignored). As she put her hand on her neck, she felt the stinging as of salt in a wound. When she looked at her hand there was a dull red smudge of blood on it. Beside where she slept in the moist earth was left, more a signature than a true spoor, one clear imprint of a wolf's paw. She erased it quickly with her hand.

Green land began to give way to black rock, scarps and canyons shelving ever upward, and at last they saw, bathed in a blue luminous haze that made it seem to float, Ascarius' keep, set on a pinnacle of dull black rock. Sunlight drew streaks of light along its walls as if by some magic, the material had become vitrified. Only a narrow trail spiraled upward, easily defended, yet no defender appeared and they climbed with impunity, wind licking at their hair and the manes of the horses.

"Don't you have the feeling that the castle rises even as we climb toward it?" asked Quickspur.

"Yea, and looking down seems to confirm it. The ground is leagues away now. Perhaps we were rash—" Hard fingers began to tickle her, and she struggled to be free of them and almost fell out of Sable's saddle and all that vast way to the ground. The same invisible hands kept her from falling and straightened her in the saddle. A moist whisper in her ear began to make obscene suggestions.

Another voice speaking from the air beside them interrupted. "Welcome to my domain. It has been most amusing, watching your futile struggles to arrive here, and there will be more festivities to come, I promise."

Arcana saw light like blue needles surround Quickspur, his horse, shooting from Sable's bowed neck, from the fingers of her hands. And she could not move. Though her perceptions still seemed to work, she felt as if time had stopped for her, the wind frozen against her face. She knew that, if Ascarius chose, he could keep them thus for always. as the daystar dimmed to a pitted fire-coal, as the cliffs eroded, lost their diamond edges and collapsed into soft black earth. As she was possessed by this knowledge, she felt herself floating airy as a bubble (and as fragile). She didn't know about Quickspur, for her perceptions were fading as she floated upward, so lightly as if she would bump gently against the translucent blue porcelain of sky.

The floating sensation was gone, and she felt immensely heavy at first, but was immediately glad to have her senses, her mind and her body returned to her. She was sitting in a large chair, the arms of which were carved (or so she thought) in the likeness of serpents. As she watched, the coils twitched and writhed, twining about her arms . Ascarius was sitting in a companion chair (the arms static) opposite her, looking much as he had in the scrying glass, except im-

mensely pleased with himself. His fingers fumbled in air for a
moment as if seeking something lost in a pouch, and he retrieved a
heavy golden goblet. "Drink this," he said, "a draught of reviving
wine." When she looked down at her hands he made another gesture so rapidly his fingers seemed to blur and the serpents straightened into chair arms again. To gain time she sipped the wine slowly
and tried to engage the sorcerer in conversation.

"Foolish, foolish. You should have realized when I pirated your
demon that my magic is superior to yours. Ah we shall have some
good games together, games of cat and mouse, of falcon and pigeon."

"I wish you'd call off your bedamned incubus. I can still feel
him, hovering around, breathing on me."

"Oh, he's taken quite an interest in his work. He finds you very
exciting."

"All things considered, I can't say I'm flattered." She made a gesture as to remove something repellent, something clinging.

"We mustn't spoil his diversion."

"At least you could release Quickspur. He won't afford you any
amusement."

"On the contrary. I'm sure he will be vastly entertaining on the
field of combat." He waved his hand and an armored knight strode
into the room, his joints creaking maddeningly. But there was something wrong about the sound, the way he moved. Suddenly the visor
flipped up with a clang, opening upon empty air. "I ween he will
find this a true test of his knighthood. Unfortunately, the end of the
tourney is in no doubt; he'll find no vulnerable spot in this perfect
knight." The suit stalked out, inhabited by nothing more than an
implacable sense of purpose.

"What of Ermintrude—She's done nothing to cause harm."

"Oh no, nothing to cause harm. Oh no." A wild look came into
the magician's eyes. "She's securely behind walls and will stay so. I
will admit I blundered in bringing her here, but how was I to know?
Oh she's quite safe, quite safe. And now, I give you the freedom of
my castle. Unfortunately, it's not untenanted, in fact, it's crowded,

with my demons." He made himself disappear, from the feet up, in a leisurely way that made Arcana fume with jealousy. Some day she might have learned to do that, if she hadn't gone out will he nill he, like a certain hotheaded knight.

N o sooner was Ascarius gone than she felt a body pressing against her own, lips set delicately, lingeringly, against her throat and clever fingers working at the fastenings of her clothing. The hands were clinging and pervasive; she felt a far-off languor stealing toward her. When she closed her eyes, the body felt solid enough. Eyes squeezed shut, she kicked. And was rewarded by solid connection with flesh and bone and a muffled grunt of pain. He had been too involved in his games to dematerialize. Still in darkness, she located the clinging, stroking hands, caught them by solid wrists and tore them from her, pushing herself away in a stumbling run. Once into the corridor she ran to more purpose, hearing hollow footsteps pursuing.

Along the passageway there was a narrow, doorless opening; she almost missed it in her flight. Wheeling around she fled into it and almost found herself falling upward against a flight of naked stone steps that led steeply and crookedly upward.

"If there's a donjon above, that may be where he's imprisoned Ermintrude." She climbed. This seemed to be an odd time to be thinking of rescuing someone else. but her head buzzed and sputtered and she found it hard to think logically. There had been a note of . . . something . . . in Ascarius' voice when he spoke of the Demoiselle, and he had said she was "safely" imprisoned. She fetched up against a great wooden door banded in metal. A tiny slot at eyelevel allowed her to peer inside. She saw a girl of pale ethereal beauty, tight golden ringlets standing around her head in a filmy halo, her dress of yellow silk drooping petal-like around her as she sat, chin on fist, beside a barred window. One heavy wooden bar held the door. and Arcana tried to force it upward. At last she worked it free, worrying that her strength appeared to be waning and wondering why she should feel so drained and listless. As she entered the cell.

Ermintrude looked up out of immense glassy blue eyes. "Who are you, Good Sir?"

"I've come to release you."

"Oh bless you." Her eyes shimmered, magnified by tears. "I don't know why Ascarius was so mean to lock me up here in this cold metal place when he knows I'm too weak and helpless to do him any harm. I was as nice to him as I knew how to be, both to him and to that nice friend of his that nobody can see; well, this is how he treats me."

Arcana looked around and saw that indeed the prison was sheathed in plates of lead. She couldn't imagine why, but it was getting harder for her to link one thought with another.

"I thank you prettily, Good Young Sir. Though I had waited and hoped that a gallant knight—no matter." She made a little curtsy.

"There is a knight below," said Arcana, "who came to rescue you."

"How *exciting!*" She put her hands together in front of her face.

"Come, we'll search for him together." Arcana ran her hand across her eyes for she had gone through a mesh of cobwebs and her vision was burning and blurring. Odd, but there were no strands of cobweb there. "Drugged wine," she shouted aloud. "For sooth, I am a very babe in Ascarius' sight." Ermintrude was descending the staircase, a dollop of sunlight, growing larger, growing smaller. Arcana teetered at the top of the stairs and would have gone toppling over except that someone caught her and swung her up, one arm under her shoulders, one under her knees. Surefootedly he descended the stairs. "Safe" she thought and her eyes opened. No one carried her; she floated on empty air like a conjurer's trick. She could see no face but that didn't stop her from tearing it with her nails. There was a stifled yelp, and with a jolt, she found herself sitting on the floor. She scrambled to her feet and began to run, but it was in the way one runs in dreams, drenched in fear-sweat over something, one knows not what, that always pursues, and feet sliding through leaden sliminess, trying one's best to run, but going nowhere. She found herself running more freely and shouted in exhilaration. The walls of the passage narrowed and burned with a velvet violet light. She burst through into noonday, feeling light as air and unencumbered, floating upward, but why——? She stopped, looked backward (and downward) in her flight. She became confused to see her heavy earthen body lying in a crumpled posture, the mouth slackly open, the eyes closed. But why such a clumsy body of dull earth-bound hues when she saw herself milky pale and filled with coruscating light of rainbow color. She was so light she could bound above the trees. She looked more closely as she passed over their branching tops, but they were not tree-like at all, but had a cauliflower texture and were dusted with a glistening greenish powder that gave them a fungoid appearance.

Below, something invisible was lifting the body and bearing it away. She would have thought she had died except that the mouth and hands moved in drunken protest. And she could feel herself (when she concentrated on it) being carried. So she was not dead, only separated. And she remembered being in this state once before while experimenting with a potion she had read of in a scroll halfeaten by worms. Ascarius had played the fool this time, for she was in demonland and free of her clinging earthshape, but not totally free, for she could feel herself being lowered to the softness of a bed.

She seemed to need no direction in this land where fungoid trees rose in minutes, collapsing as rapidly, falling in upon themselves with a gust of shining green powder, beneath an immense red sun that stood always at noon, casting down a shadowless light. She met a shape like a wavering pillar of smoke. "Arcana, I never thought to see you again."

"Ungratefulness, I call it," she said, hovering over him, an opalescent light now and again sending out a streamer of anger.

The smokewisp shrugged, though without shoulders it was hard to recognize the gesture. "How could I help it? His magic overshadows yours. Even out of the body when you meet him mind to mind, he will surely defeat you." In this shadowless land a dim coolness slid over them and looking above, Arcana saw a great black cloud gathering, lightnings playing along its flanks. In the real world her clothes were being removed garment by garment, invisible hands gloating over the bare flesh. She felt herself struggle weakly, held in the jesses of the drug, then she shrugged it off her conscious-ness as a horse twitches away a fly.

Ascarius was speaking from the cloud. "I did not know you could go out of the body with such facility. I meant only to allow my demon a little pleasure. I would have watched with interest. But perhaps this is better—mind against mind, demon against demons." The innards of the cloud swirled as if it were birthing a tornado. "Who? How? Don't look at me so out of those cow eyes. Stop mak-ing them go so blank, and for the gods' sakes suck in that pouting rosy little lip."

"It's the thing," said the Demon.

"Thing?" said Arcana with a dawning awareness.

"I don't know what it is, really, a geas, perhaps. It is a terrible blank chaos that works to suck up Ascarius' power like a sponge."

"Come now, Child. I'm not really an 'old meanie.' Let me re-turn you to your tower room. Don't dart about so!"

Arcana shot upward into the center of the thundercloud. Mind clashed against mind, and she felt an alien chill, tasting the length of his life, the *otherness* of it. Fear flashed and anger rumbled, and Arcana felt his wrath strike her like acid rain, burning, pitting, scar-ring, so that she knew after this battle she would be irrevocably changed.

The demon's lips made snail-tracks across her breasts, his hands ran like fiery silk along her thighs. Chemically cocooned in anger and pleasure. she could only move as in a bad dream. Her mind felt Ascarius' death grip weaken, and she reaffirmed her own more sol-idly. "Truce," he called then. "You yellow-headed witch. I am de-stroyed!"

Arcana did not dare trust him in a truce, not when his power so overtowered her own. Her teeth were on his windpipe and she could not let go.

"Treachery!" he said in the thinnest of wind sounds, for he was dispersing, boiling, disappearing, and the red sun was burning through his grimy tatters .

Arcana's Demon backed away from the scarlet helix that had been coiling around and through him. and watched it, too, disappear. She and the Demon did a floating, bounding dance of joy. Then she remembered herself: "The incubus!"

"We can dispel him now," suggested the Demon.

"We can't leave me in a state like that," said Arcana. "No, we'll have to let him finish, and—"

Like a shapeless bird she dived downward. through enclosing gloom, through the violet fires, entering with a wrenching click in time to experience the penultimate madness, the violent release, the floating warmth.

Awakening later, all in one piece, she watched light and shadow moving on the ceiling. She was alone, the incubus dispersed. She began to collect things that were scattered, her cast-aside clothing littering the floor. She collected Ermintrude who was still asking what had happened to the eccentric old granther with the fetching eyes. Unfortunately, or fortunately (who ever knew?), Ermintrude's wits were permanently fled to the four winds and could never be gathered. They went out into the courtyard, fearful that Quickspur's limbs would be what must needs be gathered next. He lay on the cobbles, as one dead, his armor sorely dented, but upon surveying the scene, Arcana saw lying here and there the component parts of Ascarius' perfect knight. Quickspur sat up suddenly, pushing up his visor. "He wasn't human, but I kept bashing away at him till one part fell off and then another. He was a hell of a fightingman, I thought, till I found out there wasn't anyone in there at all, just a suit of armor that walked like a man.

At that point he saw Ermintrude, her small hands clasped in adoration and the most appalling blankness in her blank blue eyes. "My lady," he intoned, rising only to kneel to her feet. He gingerly picked up the hem of her skirt and pressed it to his lips. "I know I am all unworthy to touch a hair on your lovely head or to beg a smile from your pearl-like teeth, but if you'll allow it, I'll return you to your father, defending you to the death, if need be."

Arcana sat in a dank chamber of the catacombs where Ascarius practiced his sorcery. She banged the lute and chanted in a nasal voice. "Oh my heart is laden. Oh my heart is full of—"

"Oh my ears are broken," echoed a still small voice above the faded pentagram that Ascarius had chalked on the floor. "Fair Demoiselle, is your heart truly broken?" chuckled the demon.

She felt for it, as to check an it were still pumping. "I think not. But to think that Quickspur—that lout will depart not even knowing that I am a woman and that I lay next to him all those nights we searched so long. If I told him now it would naught but scare him out of his iron pants. Besides, he has eyes for Ermintrude only."

"Her eyes are mirrors in which he sees himself as he wishes to be seen. Have you any sorceries as strong as that?" She twanged the lute at him, snapping a string that curled up in a discordant sound. "That incubus—he couldn't have been you by any chance?"

Muted retching sounds.

"I was wondering, but—Good, we shall pack up all Ascarius' books, gredients and magicks. I will learn all that he knew, and then—"

"You will attempt to rule the world," said the Demon approvingly. "To control the ocean tides and the four winds."

"I was thinking more of summoning the incubus." The Demon reeled out pale tentacles of angry smoke as she dived behind a workbench, her sardonic laughter hanging demonlike in empty air.

Morrien's Bitch

The camp slept, each man rolled in his blanket like a corpse as the fires burned down and banked themselves into mounds of coals lit red from within. Riska crept among the sleeping soldiers, crouching to diminish her silhouette. She rummaged among one of the packs, her fingers deftly choosing what she wanted: two coins of a dull metal, a packet of dried meat, a loaf of black bread, hard cheese—the kinds of rations she had grown sick of in the past few months. There was a hoarse shout as a passing sentry discovered her and cried out, his alert tinged with a superstitious fear which delighted her. The men about her were stirring, sitting up, reaching for swords and bows. She didn't panic. She shouldered her swag-pouch and began to run. Though she was soon pursued, she moved at a measured jogging pace. She leaped from the lip of a dry riverbed, caught hold of stringy underbrush to keep from falling all the way down. Where the bank was steeply undercut, a tangle of brush hid an opening like an animal's den. Into this she slid. One man saw the brush spring back and tried to follow. He squirmed through the opening and along a narrow burrow that ended in a wall of root-grown earth. Puzzled, he backed out to confront the laughter of his companions.

Not so deep in earth that she couldn't hear this laughter, Riska paused, and smiled, her hand on the lever, then continued on down the slanting corridor now large enough for her to walk upright. She came at last to a chamber and touched a boss on the wall to flood the room with hazy blue light, illuminating the contents: a melange of richly ornate furniture and art objects more like the collection of a pack rat than a room for human habitation. She gnawed listlessly at the bread and cheese, paying little attention to the wealth surrounding her.

"A ghost! My men in the field seeing ghosts?"

The aide looked properly chastened as Morrien paced the length of the room, looking as if he'd like to drive his fist through something solid, possibly the aide's face. "It roams the camp, usually by night, though some claim to have seen it skulking about early in the morning. It's nothing serious, not a threat, except that it damages morale. And it takes things, sir."

Morrien thrust his face toward the sweating countenance of the aide. "A ghost can't take things. What you have is a garden variety thief." The aide cleared his throat uncomfortably, started to say something, then seemed to think better of it.

"What is it, man?" Morrien slapped his open palm gently with his leather gauntlets.

"It's something they don't know how to fight. It disappears."

"I'll send Dant, my Third. He'd like to make points while Kyren is off trying to squeeze some assistance out of the neighboring villages—not an errand likely to be successful, but one that's necessary for a dwindling army."

Riska became aware of the large, loud-voiced, red-faced Dant, though not by rank or name, as she continued her raids on Morrien's camp. The more she saw Dant roaring and stamping his frustrated rage, the more often she scavenged through the camp, sometimes even when she had a surfeit of food piled in her home chamber. When pursued she disappeared into a burrow or crevice in the rocks, only to appear to others on the other side of the encampment.

One night she crept boldly toward Dant's tent. Stealthily she slipped inside, lulled by raucous snoring sounds. She knelt, not breathing, her thief-clever hands busy, then she sneaked out again, zigzagging to avoid patches of moonlight. As she slid toward cover she stopped long enough to give a sleeping soldier a sharp kick. His howl of pain aroused the camp and when Riska should have been running toward her exit, a shadowy cleft in the rocks, she crouched behind a tree, watching.

With a bellow Dant came pounding from his tent. Before he had fully emerged, the rope she had tied from his leg to the pole structure that supported the tent brought tent and man down together in a satisfying cursing, struggling mass. She fled for her escape hatch and slid to a stop when she saw that it was guarded. She wheeled and made a dash toward another opening she knew, but it was too far and all the camp was now alerted. She ran well, dodging and wheeling, but was caught at last, crushed down into the dirt under two or three heavy bodies. For the second time in her life she felt real fear and not just exhilaration.

Riska awoke to darkness, her limbs bent back awkwardly. As she ran her tongue across dry lips she felt the lower one split and swollen. Her captors must have been a little over-enthusiastic. Still, except for being tied, she felt strong enough to run if need be. She rubbed her head against the ground, trying to dislodge the blindfold, but made little progress. Then she lay listening, for footsteps and voices were coming. "I had it put in my tent for the time being."

"It's human, not a spirit, believe me. Only a human would have the maliciousness to—"

Riska heard the other man laugh.

"You wouldn't find it so humorous, Kyren, if we discovered an Ultebren spy in our midst."

"Spies don't waste their time on schoolboy tricks."

Their voices were above her now and light made her eyes water as the blindfold was taken off. She recognized the red-faced Dant but not the man who was with him. He had tightly curled hair graduated in color from black to smoke to silver, and a small pointed beard. She didn't like the look of cold intelligence in his eyes.

"A spy, a spy for Amery of Ultebrel! The crest, man, the crest." Riska wore a leather tabard with the crest of Ultebren royalty worked into it.

"Put him to torture. We'll have out his secrets!"

Kyren's thin hand gripped her face and turned it into the lanternlight. "Ah no," he said. "Is that possible?" He jerked loose the ties on one side of the tabard and slid his hand inside. "Your spy is . . . a woman. No mistake."

Dant cursed without taking a breath for some moments.

"Where did you get the garment you wear?" Kyren demanded.

She looked down where his hand still moved lazily beneath the tabard. "Haven't you proved yet what you wanted to know?" She writhed a little as his fingers closed on a tender spot. Blinked back the pain. "I stole it. Up until four months ago I was a thief in Ultebre."

He leaned back, releasing her. "So you know a way into Ultebre's fortress, eh?"

"Then she's no real danger to us," said Dant. We'll give her to the men. There aren't enough women here as it is and what there are resemble hags. This one is at least young, if lacking in beauty."

"And feminine graces," said Kyren. "But we haven't solved all the mysteries. When we searched the opening in the rock through which she meant to escape, we found a series of tunnels all of which led back to the entrance again. No one could escape by this, yet she has always escaped until now."

Riska struggled to sit up. "If you promise to release me, I'll show you the secret of the caverns."

Dant moved to untie her.

"No. I for one don't want to follow her into those uncertain darknesses by night. Perhaps tomorrow."

"You're afraid?" asked Dant so bluntly that Riska wondered how someone with such a loose mouth had lived long enough to rise so high. Kyren favored him with an arrogant look that he didn't half understand, though Riska understood fully and feared for him.

Morning found her totally numb in arms and legs from being bound so tightly all night. No chance to run now, but she thought eagerly of her caverns. Once in their winding darknesses, she was master and she would find a way to repay. She was released and hauled to her feet—but without any feeling left in them, it was hard to stand. "I'll find a way to repay," she thought as she was cuffed and dragged to her feet again and thrust out of the tent. Dant was waiting outside and gave her a vicious look, evidently remembering that she had been the one to humiliate him.

"Do we have to go back to the caves?" she whined for his bene-fit. "I'm half dead with weariness, having spent most of the night showing all their secret ways, how to come and go like a ghost in the night."

"Kyren, that traitor. . . ."

"He was especially pleased that there is a hidden way into the heart of Ultebre itself so I pointed it out to him."

"He'll be off to Morrien with this news, branding me an in-competent."

"Not an incompetent, sir—fool, he said."

Dant's yeasty face seemed to swell in a ferment of anger.

And at that moment Kyren appeared cool and unsuspecting. In-nocent, of this at any rate.

Dant pulled his sword from its sheath with a sinister scraping sound. "Fool, is it? You dared to laugh at my misfortune this past night and you would say me ill with Morrien, *as you always have.*" For a moment Kyren looked surprised and Riska held her breath, afraid that ophic intelligence would strike quickly to the real cause of the quarrel. But he was a fighting man, among other men, and with a sword drawn against him. He had no other choice.

The fight lasted longer than she thought it would. She began to see why Dant had gone so high. He was a headlong, dangerous fighter. However, the outcome was no different than she had ex-pected. Kyren looked at the sprawled body with an insolent gaze and called for a cloth to wipe his sword. He cleaned it fastidiously, taking his time. She shifted from foot to foot, testing. The guard still held her by the arm, but rather loosely, his attention being grasped by the fight and now by the body of Dant. She sank her teeth into the soldier's hand. As he shouted, she twisted away, but he had a better hold than she thought and she came up hard, nearly falling.

Kyren now approached, shaking his head. She saw, with some disquiet, that he had neglected to sheathe his sword. "You betray yourself," he said, placing the edge hard against her throat and pressing it, delicately. "Dant was a fool, but in his way he was a good man and in that way, I respected him. You thought him a tool, to be used and discarded. And you didn't hesitate. Am I right?" She nodded, feeling the sword edge break the skin. If she lived, and he was fool enough to enter the caves—

He swung the weapon away, sheathed it. "You'd be dead by now if you didn't have some secret knowledge of how to enter Ultebre by stealth. Don't congratulate yourself. I'll have all your knowledge by sunset, and if you're lucky, you'll have your life. I can't promise any more than that, as you seem somewhat stubborn."

"It isn't something I can tell. I'd have to show you. I'm willing to go with my hands tied, blindfolded, if there's so much to be frightened of."

"You almost convince me, but Morrien himself is on his way; he'll be here by tomorrow. I prefer to wait for him. Tie her tightly. If you or any other man on guard duty gets lonely, remember that she's at your disposal."

"If this is important to you, and it seems to be, you'd do better not to bait and anger me. I can be stubborn, and I might manage to die without speaking.

"You take each small advantage and squeeze it dry, don't you, advancing yourself with every turn. If I can believe my ears now, the prisoner is setting the terms of her own captivity." She believed that he was as near to breaking out into overt violence as he would ever come; so wisely, she fell silent. She was pleased when she was taken to a tent and left inside unbound. Nor must her guard have felt any loneliness through the long afternoon. Morrien was conducted to the prisoner's tent by an uncharacteristically shaken Kyren.

"This is just a girl," said Morrien. "After all you've told me, I expected an ogre, at least." The prisoner looked up from where she sat on the ground.

"Get up," shouted Kyren, aiming a kick in her direction, which she avoided and rose lithely. She was not as tall as Morrien, but she was tall, long of limb and appeared to have a wiry strength unbecoming in a woman, to his way of thinking.

"I'm told you know of hidden ways into Ultebre's citadel. That you stole a garment from Amery's palace."

"I keep telling them so; and I keep offering to guide you, freely, yet all I get are threats of violence and torture." Though dark hair hung down raggedly over one eye and her mouth had a hard, sullen look to it, he could not believe all that Kyren said of her. She seemed helpless rather than ravening.

"Has she so offered?" Kyren looked down, muttered, "Yes. But I don't trust her and you shouldn't either. I think of Dant."

"If the thing was done as you say, it was cleverly done. I could admire such cleverness." The prisoner cast a triumphant glance at Kyren and warmed visibly to Morrien. He was a pleasant sight, his thick hair and beard the color of bronze, his face strongly beautiful, his heavy travel cloak adding to the width of his shoulders.

"How do you come to know these warrens?"

"They're my home. My grandfather discovered their secrets and my father taught me all there is to be known of the cavernways, No one knows who built them; they were ancient in the time of my grandfather. We used them for our own purposes."

"Thievery."

"What could be more convenient? Routes of egress opening at all points in the city, out of sewers and drains, alleyways and cisterns; there are even many passageways opening inside buildings."

"Inside the palace of my cousin Amery and the dwelling of Jos'l, his minister. I'd like to burst in on them at this moment as they gloat over expelling me from my rightful fiefdom. Amery acted as my friend while Jos'l subverted the army, bribing, and killing those who would not be bribed. When I escaped with what ragtag of an army I could keep about me, Amery captured Llana, my wife-to-be, tortured and killed her when he found her loyalty could not be bartered. I have a lot to *thank* those two for when we meet face to face, and perhaps now there's a chance we will."

"If you mean to kill Jos'l I'll be well satisfied. He's the one that signed the order—" her voice grew weak to inaudibility. By an effort she went on. "There were never enough women in the tunnels to satisfy the band of thieves my father had gathered, so the custom was to carry off women from Ultebre. But one managed to find her way back and a trap was laid. They caught all but me and a young apprentice thief who returned to his home in an outlying village. You know Jos'l's punishment for thievery."

"Impalement."

She bit her lip. "I watched from one of our secret egresses. I don't know why. I watched but there was nothing I could do." She shuddered and for all her efforts to control them, tears began sliding from her eyes. She turned away and wiped her face with the back of her hand as if she had done something shameful, then turned back to finish the story. "They guard many of the entrance ways now, though they can't penetrate deeply into them. Only I know all the turnings and a certain secret which I will show to your man, presently. I turned to the open country for survival, for I was alone and had no heart to return to the city."

"A sad story," said Kyren dryly, "if true. I'm willing to test the truth of this for you by various means of 'persuasion' which I know."

"I believe her," said Morrien, "and I don't think I'm over-trusting."

"If he doesn't believe it, let him accompany me into the caverns," said Riska.

Kyren hesitated. His cool intelligence said no, but pride struggled not to let himself admit that for some reason he feared to go with her. "Very well," he said grudgingly, "but I will take two of my best soldiers as well. And as you once agreed, you will be bound and blindfolded."

They entered a cleft in the rock. Blindfolded, Riska stumbled against a lichenous protrusion in the wall. Her cursing masked the low rumble of rock panels moving aside on metal tracks. "If you insist on my being blindfolded, at least see that I don't break my neck," she protested. They followed a narrow channel that had reportedly only circled back upon itself, yet this seemed straight enough. Cool air blew through the cavernways; it did not have the usual close dampness of a true cave. After a while Kyren noticed that the walls were smooth as if the builders no longer cared to camouflage the fact that these passageways seemed melted out of the rock.

"Who could have made these? Was there no clue?"

"My grandfather who discovered them said that the builders left nothing, except the result of their handiwork and the central core of the present city of Ultebre. Though sometimes I have searched these caverns for something they might have left behind."

"Perhaps as well they don't return, if they are as skilled in magic as this indicates."

They traveled for long hours through the tunnels. Kyren had no idea of where he might be when Riska cautioned him to quietness. The way led sharply upward. Riska must have done something, he wasn't sure what, because a door slid back in what looked like solid stone. Then they were climbing some winding stairs in what looked like a cellar half filled with rubble. A slot let through a spangle of outerworld light and Kyren set his eyes to it, unsure. Tall, fluted pillars held the roof up grandly and the walls rippled with lush tapestries, all worked in battle scenes in which the Ultebren crest was prominently displayed.

"The palace itself!" said Kyren, in his excitement forgetting himself and pulling her close. "Is there a way to enter?"

"Yes. I don't know whether or not it was discovered. We seldom used it because there were so many guards in the palace."

"If an army broke through here—and at other strategic spots in the city. . . . Let's go back. Morrien must know."

At some point in the unrelieved darkness, Kyren saw Riska bound ahead, disappearing around a sharp turn in the tunnel. He shouted to his soldiers to pursue; but beyond the turn, the cavern seemed to take a different direction than before, though Kyren couldn't be sure, having negotiated it but once. No sign of her ahead in the dimness, and now other openings were appearing to right and left.

A soldier dared say what Kyren would not. "We're lost."

"She waited. The she-vulture waited until she had me in her hands. I'll be your guide willingly, she said and must have laughed to herself in the saying." They wandered together in darkness. After a certain length of time it was no longer a seeking out of the right route but a shambling in blind despair. Trickles of water that seeped through the walls and down onto the floor quenched their thirst, but even the drive for survival withered against cool smooth stone, echoing silence and everlasting darkness. "She's buried us alive," said Kyren, as his thoughts circled endlessly in dreams of sound and light. "She simply walked off and left us here without a further thought, without any idea of mercy."

"She's but a semblance of a woman over the soul of a wolf-bitch," said a soldier ruefully as he scooped up tepid water from a runnel in the floor.

"I wonder what exquisite lie she'll tell Morrien."

"You think she'll go back there?"

"You should have seen her with Morrien. If ever bitch-wolf craved a master—"

"So much the worse for him if he's been chosen. But that changes nothing for us."

Images of the grave tormented Kyren as even his anger banked and all but went out. They huddled in a cul-de-sac in the rocks, their strength having given out. One of their number had fallen into delirium. Kyren wondered idly, "If one of us dies before the others—"

A vision came to him of peeling a strip of flesh off a human thigh, of putting it to his lips. He groaned audibly and did not dare to put the obscene idea into words. But if one grew very hungry—the idea taunted him. He grew a little weaker from the mental conflict. His head drooped to his knees as if his skull were a heavy pod on a thin reed, drying toward autumn. The air that drifted through was cool, the silence complete. He did not know how long she had been standing there. It didn't seem to matter, for he was too weak to try to kill her even if he could remember what he wanted to kill her for. She drew near; her hair and clothing held the smells of sunlight and vegetation; there was a slip of something green caught on her trousers. Like a baby he reached toward it.

She was helping him rise, then the others. "You were lost," she said persuasively, hypnotically into his ear as she guided him out of the blind tunnel. "I searched and searched. Then I reported it to Morrien. I returned after these many days to make a final search."

"He believed you?"

"Hard to say. No one was there to discount my story. I told him you abandoned me in the caverns, bound and blind-folded, once you decided you knew the way to Ultebre, but in your haste to return you took a wrong turning. Fortunately for me, a blindfold was an aid my father used to teach me the tunnels' windings. The story seemed likely enough, considering that you wanted to abandon me all along, isn't that right?"

His head swam. He could rage inwardly and swear to himself that Morrien would know the truth, but he could say nothing aloud, for he was in her hands, faint with hunger and paralyzed with fear that he would never see the light again.

"I'm not sure it matters what version of the story you tell him, for you will have to tell him that you have gone into the undefended heart of Ultebre. If he truly wants his revenge, then he, all of you, will have to stomach me as best you can."

Light and sound and the prosaic bustle of everyday life returned as they left the caverns, and Kyren began to doubt that she had done him a kindness in saving his life. They said that Kyren was like a man returned from the dead. They said also that after this time he was changed, that his nerve had been broken. In Kyren's absence Morrien had named Riska his Second, almost as a joke (the men said Morrien's bitch and laughed), but Kyren never disputed it. Though he hinted and said things by indirection, he never was able to tell Morrien to his face how he feared for him.

With Riska's guidance Morrien had several reconnaissance parties sent through to Ultebre. They found one entrance guarded but lackadaisically by a guard who seemed to consider his post a sinecure and spent most of his time napping or playing a game with painted strips of wood. The last patrol that returned brought a captive. "Our tunnel opened into the women's quarters," explained the leader. "We brought you a memento." He pushed forward a shivering girl dressed in a gauzy skirt and some strategically placed jewelry. "She says her name is Gisela. She's one of Amery's latest concubines, no doubt."

"I'm a dancer," said the girl sulkily. "The best in Ultebre."

"I warned them the trouble our band had when it started carrying off women," said Riska, but in his inspection of Gisela, Morrien ignored her completely. Kyren would have recognized and feared the expression on her face had he been there to see it.

"Dismissed," he said to the soldiers, looking at Riska to include her. They were in Morrien's chambers, and Riska, as Second, occupied a room adjacent to them.

Gisela, once she had smoothed her rumpled skirt, seemed to make herself at home, obviously enjoying Morrien's gaze on her.

"Get rid of her," said Riska with a sound of disgust.

Morrien looked over at her, half-smiling as if amused by what he'd heard. Riska was always difficult to get along with but she'd never given him a direct order and he didn't look as if he wanted her to start now.

She met his look angrily, directly. "In this place you'll bed me and no other." Morrien looked at Gisela, her eyes bright and comprehending, and felt almost embarrassed at Riska's bluntness.

"I don't want *you*," he said, returning plain speech for bluntness, putting a wealth of disgust in that last word.

"Do you want Amery's life—and Jos'l's? And all their tribe? Do you want to see their blood run at your feet, their faces bloated in death?" She was dark of eyes and olive of skin but she could blaze with a dark radiance.

He made an abrupt gesture, sending Gisela scuttling from the room. Not that he was afraid of the outcome of this confrontation—not that at all—if Riska insisted on humiliating herself. . . .

"Behind my back they call me she-wolf and sewer-rat. I don't mind the names. In a way they're true—but you need me. Above ground your pitiful army would be defeated. In the caverns, with me to lead, you can appear anywhere you choose. If you tried to explore for yourself it could take half a lifetime and in the meantime

Amery and Jos'l despoil Ultebre at their leisure."

He advanced on her until they were nearly eye to eye. "You'd command me to your bed with revenge as the price. Are you so . . . desperate as all that?"

"I'm only practical. I find you attractive and it seems unlikely that I'd have my way with you under normal circumstances, being thought savage in appearance—not that I'm not satisfied with how I look, you understand."

He felt his hold on his temper began to loosen. What kind of unnatural bitch was this—any other woman would have been dissolved in tears by now. Perhaps if she had, he might have been persuaded to give the comfort she sought, but not ordered, not under threats.

She watched his hand twitch toward a knife on a belt he wasn't wearing. "Killing me wouldn't solve anything. I'm very much afraid there's but one answer." She reclined on a dais covered in furs. She seemed to enjoy the anger that came and went across his face, as he struggled for control. She had great faith in his self control.

To continue their eye-to-eye confrontation, he had to bend down over the dais. "You might, in some ways I know, be persuaded to lead us about the caverns." He put the balls of his thumbs gently on her eyelids. "One doesn't need eyes underground, for example." She drew away slightly, then regained her composure. "You would find me stubborn, I'm afraid, and afterward a very confused guide. I might even leave you to wander the tunnels till you died."

Silence for some moments.

He threw himself down onto the dais beside her. "What are you trying to do? Do you want to bring me to my knees, carry me off, rape me? He lay on the dais, hands beneath his head, half-joking, half in a kind of confusion. "Here I am, helpless, in your hands. Go ahead. I'll be very interested to see how you accomplish it."

She could not suppress a laugh. She put her hand gently on his chest. "I don't say I wouldn't like to, if it were possible, but I believe we'd find it awkward. No, I'll abide by tradition in this."

He made a sudden movement, more menacing than anything

else. "Very friendly, very gently," she cautioned. "Treat me as you intended to treat her. You can even pretend I'm Gisela, I don't mind." He tried, closing his eyes as he kissed her when all his instincts were screaming for blood. He fantasized snapping her scrawny neck, doing other unprintable things. When the kiss was ended, she drew back, a mocking smile on her lips. "You're a disappointing lover. I release you. You're free to go to your little Gisela." He blinked.

Had she changed her mind, finding this whole process too degrading, or was she playing the kinds of power games he found so amusing when she played them against other people. For some moments he was blind, deaf, dumb with anger; but as usual, she had calculated the limits of his control. She always calculated everything to a hair's tolerance, but it was possible that this time she had overextended herself a bit.

"You may go," she was saying and attempting to roll sideways off the dais. He gave a sudden, blood-curdling war cry, following it immediately with another even shriller. Anyone who heard it would think that he had gone (or been sent) over the edge. She shrank back into herself a little, but recovered well.

"I'm mad with love, Gisela," he said, scrabbling after her over the mounded furs. "My lovely, my golden one."

"Morrien, wake up." She caught him on the side of the head with an open handed blow that made his ears ring, perhaps as a gesture to bring him to his senses. They tumbled from the dais as he grappled with her. For her lesser size, she really wasn't bad as a fighter, he noted; it was all be could do to restrain her and undo the strings of her tabard. He kept a glassy look in his eyes and kept on mumbling mindless things about Gisela. She could only blame herself that she had pushed him too far and driven him to this (or so he hoped). He twined his fingers in her hair in the pretext of caressing it and brought her head down smartly against the stone floor, not enough for damage, just enough to stop this infernal wrestling match. He hoped she hadn't presence of mind left to realize how premeditated that act seemed. Her eyes went a little blank and he could do anything he wanted, so for awhile he did, though it wasn't

as enjoyable as he'd hoped. Then he gave her what she had professed
to want, but not friendly, not gentle as she had ordered. All with the
excuse of his feigned madness, though possibly by that time he had
achieved a kind of madness of his own, and perhaps he would never
be sure at this point just who had been raped.

Riska limped a little as she led the way into the tunnel and when
she moved, she moved carefully. "I had some terrible dreams last
night," he said, glad that the darkness masked his expression; he
could not have taunted her so in the light.

"Your dreams are not my concern," she said coldly. "I slept . . .
well. What is it you remember of your dream?"

"I dreamed of an enemy. Someone I wanted to kill."

"Sorry." He enjoyed the way she recoiled when he accidentally
bumped against her, but, as he was beginning to realize with more
and more clarity, he must not carry these games too far. She was not
stupid and with the least flicker of suspicion, she would leave him
here to wander about until he died. She'd probably enjoy the idea of
it.

Morrien crouched at the opening into the palace. His nerves
were pulled tight by the waiting. His troops were in position at the
hundred egresses of Ultebre. Down the tunnelways the word was
passed. "Down the tyrant, Amery." Ultebre, the queen city, was almost in their hands. Morrien burst out amidst general confusion;
Riska had insisted she be at his side, as Second. He didn't object;
perhaps some enthusiastic Ultebren would settle his dilemma by
killing her. Though he supposed he would regret her death. Here,
even in the palace itself, defense was poorly organized. He supposed
their strength had been concentrated along the walls with their tur-
rets and wonderful war machines, unfortunately now facing the
wrong way for a proper defense.

His sword was drawn, but he saw little combat, his troops going
before him, so easily it seemed, putting to rout the confused palace
guard. He kept hearing the plaintive question, "Where are they all
coming from?" *Like insects from the walls and rats from the sewers,* he

thought. An inner chamber was fiercely guarded and Morrien joined in the close fighting, thinking that perhaps Amery was here. The defense cut down or scattered, they battered down the door. Amery's body lay sprawled across some cushions. His guard had given him the time to be quite dead, but hardly peaceful looking, the skin cyanotic, flecks of foam drying around the mouth.

"He was wise," observed Morrien.

"Cut off the head," said Riska. "Have it displayed on a pike at the city's gate. The body you can throw into the sewers for the rats to squabble over." Soldiers rushed to carry this out, as a messenger entered to tell them that Jos'l had escaped, gotten out of the city in the confusion of its fall. "Then don't waste time standing here puling. Get the word out—one hundred gold pieces for the return of Jos'l . . . alive."

Kyren and Morrien exchanged looks as she left. "Now that we are in control, the savage is of no further use. She is a positive danger. And you know it well."

Morrien gave a gesture of dismissal, but Kyren caught his eye and a look of understanding passed between them.

After many days had passed Riska confronted the guards at the door of the fine new house that Morrien had provided for her. They crossed their pikes as she approached. "Your ladyship is not to go out alone," said one of them. "The streets still hold some danger. The conquest of the city still goes on in isolated areas."

She laughed rudely. Though the sound of it made him shuffle in embarrassment, it didn't change the position of the pikes.

"Say I do not go out . . . by Morrien's order."

She wheeled about and walked disconsolately through the richly furnished rooms. At first this seemed a part of what she had won. There had been parties; Morrien had even been here once though he had looked rather grim. The baths, the servants, the fine clothes, these had distracted her somewhat. But it hadn't taken her that long to realize that no matter how fine the quarters, when you couldn't leave them, you were in prison. And Morrien's grim face might mean more than responsibility for reorganizing the government of Ultebre.

The assassin was dressed in dark clothing so he was halfway across her bed chamber before she detected him. Her only warning was the light rippling down the knife blade. His hand arched back, down, struck the mounded fabric on the dais. It was not really luck that she had decided to sleep on the floor. He was just discovering that he had murdered the bedclothes when she hit him from behind with a brass lamp. She turned him over with a foot, but didn't recognize him, though she had had a fleeting hope when she had struck him that it would be Kyren, and an unexpressed fear that it was Morrien. She shouted and threw the lamp against the wall with a metallic crash. When the guard entered, he tripped over the sprawled body of the assassin and called out for his companion as she had hoped. As they crouched over the assassin, she slipped from the room and made for the unguarded door, no longer a fine lady, nor a prisoner, but free and everything they thought her—perhaps even worse.

Morrien entered his sleeping chamber wearily, releasing his cloak from his shoulders to let it fall on the floor. A servant rushed to attend him, but Morrien spoke curtly, sending him away.

A dagger struck the inlaid wood of the floor and vibrated rattlingly between Morrien and Riska, who stepped from the shadows. "I came to return this," she said and lifted her lip off white teeth in a smile.

He still had a knife at his belt, if he wished to draw it, but he seemed oblivious of the weapon. "It seemed the only solution. I only wanted you in a safe place, out of the way, but Kyren—"

"You knew he hated me. You knew what he would do."

"I don't know. I suppose so. I had even thought of making you my lady, to rule with me." There was a silence as their eyes met, then Riska broke it with a laugh that Morrien joined in.

"I see. The allies one makes in war can become an embarrassment in time of peace. Times change and people do not." She turned to go.

"I will have to set men to exploring the caverns. I can't be as blissfully ignorant of history as Amery was."

"Their windings are many and deep, and I know secrets by which the very walls may be changed. It will be long before you may say you have found them all out. And a human life is short."

"All things considered, yours may be shorter than most."

"Perhaps . . . if you don't guard the ways too strongly, you may waken to someone who will lie down with you—like someone who comes in a dream. In the morning, some trinket or some treasure may be missing. I hear there are thieves in Ultebre."

Screaming to get Out

The city shone with a gauzy sleazy phosphorescence as things do in the later stages of decay. He could move through it, unthinking, unfeeling, in perfect safety, and though a lot had happened to make him what he was, at this moment he might as well have existed forever in this state, a suspension between blind exaltation and despair. But it must not be imagined that he knew this about himself any more than a rat is aware of its own prowess in the gritty levels just above bare survival. If it paused to consider, it would no longer be a rat. He cruised in the dark, anonymous car until he felt the hunger come on him. That last one had been good. He remembered her face, ugly even before the tears streaked it and made her eyes red and swollen and her expression, that of an animal suffering and not knowing the reason why.

"You're like the Kleenex I blow my nose into," he had said. She had pulled a sheet over her nakedness. Her body was ugly, too, bony and underdeveloped. He always chose the ugly ones. They seemed his legitimate prey in a world that worshipped physical beauty. She had started crying then in a satisfying way, the half-repressed, agonized sound of an adult's crying. Her inner self was as unattractive as the rest of her; no resources there, though she had probably been told at some point in her life that plain girls had "character." He had called her a couple of appropriate names and left, whistling down the street past the crumbling façades of the buildings, the castoffs of a technological society, the skeleton of a ruined bike, rusty blades of an electric fan, beer cans, and got into the car as one shoulders into a comfortable garment. The torn and sagging seat accommodated itself to his weight and the motor coughed into tenuous life.

He had read about her later in the paper. How she had closed all the windows and doors and turned on the gas. That was icing on the

106

cake to him. The landlady (nosy old bag) had smelled the gas and had gone upstairs just in time to save her. That was even better, he thought. Let her live, that was the ticket. A suicide that failed was even better than one that succeeded. He had felt sated for days after that one, and was almost chary of trying again because the next one might not measure up.

Even though with each encounter it seemed he carried something away, it must not be thought that he did what he did with any malice. That it was something he could do and so did was all the explanation there was.

He drove up to a drive-in restaurant and watched the car hops go in and out with clockwork precision, parading their majorette legs in white short-shorts. They were safe from him and showed little interest in waiting on him, choosing instead the cars that spilled over with wise-cracking, rude-talking boys. He left the car and went inside and sat at a table where he ordered a coffee and drank it in measured sips. No one noticed him particularly because he wore that best of all disguises in the city, a face like everyone else's. Only the expressions moving quickly across his face at times insinuated a deformity of the spirit.

He looked around the room. Even though the place had a surface semblance of shining newness, a careful eye could see everywhere the signs of decay and ultimate fall. Corrosion had begun to eat in a circular pattern under the table's metal feet on the shining pseudo-marble tiles. There were burn scars where someone's cigarette had melted the gleaming black plastic tabletop. But he really didn't see these things as individual phenomena, because he himself was a part of the larger phenomenon which was slowly eating the city and all the people, its component parts.

She was behind the counter so that only half her bulk was visible, stomach rising to meet the pendulous breasts straining the white fabric of her uniform, chins, stacked one upon the other, sloping downward like tallow melting, features a distorted blur of protruding cheeks, doughy white skin, tiny wise eyes like something peering out, a prisoner beneath the weight of all that gross flesh. What was it they always said about a thin person screaming to get out? He ran his tongue rapidly across his lips. She moved serenely like some huge sea beast, and she had deft, seemingly boneless white hands that worked swiftly, almost with a life of their own.

Like him, she too was able to be what she was without thinking about it. As she worked, her white hands lifted toward her face, French fries dripping with oil, sandwiches oozing mayonnaise, candy bars richly coated with chocolate, hiding in their centers crunchy, oily nuts. Although she did not bother to wonder why she was allowed to eat up this much of the profits, the manager was able to figure up how much he made on a worker who was never sick, never late, never complained and who worked untiringly at substandard wages. She did not wonder about it because she did not realize she was eating all these things. She lived almost every waking minute with a hunger that was a dull ache inside her and seemed to have nothing whatever to do with the rich foods her hands were continually putting into her mouth. Sometimes she tried to think about herself, who she was, but she could only feel herself as a mouth, empty and salivating for something, she didn't know what.

He studied her heavy body as she moved back and forth behind the counter. What must she look like naked: an outre Buddha, shaped by dirty hands from a wad of dough, then allowed to rise . . . and rise. He smiled at the thought, and she orbited toward him, greasy patches shining on forehead and cheeks.

"D'you want it warmed up?"

"What?"

"Your coffee."

"Oh. Yeah. Business slow tonight?"

And she started, all the way through the layers of fat, as though she wasn't used to having anyone notice that she was human, let alone address a remark to her, let alone a man!

"Yeah, yeah, it is," she said in a small, strangely unresonant voice. They looked at each other, each seeming to awaken from a sleep. There was a meeting here, as of two large though dormant powers, testing strength, then each subsided and for the moment slept again.

He toyed with the coffee cup, playing at self-consciousness, "What time do you get off work? I suppose it's late."

"About twelve."

"Is it . . . all right if I pick you up? It's just that I . . . get lonely sometimes. You know how it is." And he knew that she did know.

"Okay."

He put money on the table and left hastily, not sure that he would be back. He sensed a strength in her where there should be nothing but weakness. Well, he didn't have to come back, not if he didn't want to.

She allowed her hands to attend unerringly to her tasks, unaware of everything except the hunger that now seemed to intensify. She never understood it, and tried to appease it by eating, but it rarely went away.

Rain began to tap insistent fingernails against the plate glass. The car hops squealed and ran for cover, and since it was getting late, the manager let them go home. They laughed and chattered among themselves, then scattered into the wet night. To her they were alien creatures. She could not imagine their lives, and she couldn't remember ever having been as young as they were. She didn't try very hard to recall. There was a dim memory of a damp, dark, closed-in space. She stopped trying to remember and thought instead of the nice young man. Her mind spiraled out into the rainy night as though willing him to come back.

The windshield wipers worked violently against the torrent of wind-driven rain. Not even rain could cleanse the city; the stuff in the air polluted the rain, giving it a chemical smell; the water in the gutters was brown, yearning toward sewers that underlay the city in myriad dark channels. He eased the car into one of the parking stalls before the deserted drive-in. The place looked haunted with its girls departed, its neons blinked out. He thought for a moment that she hadn't waited, then he saw the bulk of her outlined in the dim glow from a street lamp.

The rain didn't matter to her; she walked toward him placidly as if she didn't feel it. Her ponderous form was grotesque, draped in a wrinkled tan raincoat and her sparse hair hung around her face in limp strands. Then she was inside the car. He felt the seat go down the extremity of its springs. She brought with her the smell of wet hair, wet clothing and some other scent, not really unpleasant, not perfume. He was suddenly comfortable in her presence, as though her size was something to lean against.

"A good thing I came back for you. You'd get soaked walking home. You need someone to take care of you." That line always appealed to them. "What's your address?"

"415 Fenwick."

"That's quite a ways. Do you walk every night after dark?"

"Yeah."

"I'd think you'd be afraid."

"I'm not." A statement of fact.

The car was one of the few on the rainblack street. Water was dashed across the windshield and hissed under the tires. She didn't speak further but sat, imposing and imperturbable. It should have made him nervous, but somehow it didn't. For all her weight she didn't seem quite real. It was as though he might look away for a moment and look back to find her gone.

He entered her street. The buildings sagged subtly one against the other, their façades crumbling off in layers. Gaping stars in windowpanes attested to emptiness. "Have you lived in this neighborhood long?

She stopped and tried to think. "I've lived here . . . all my life," she said, surprised to realize that it was true. White bodies writhing and the beginning of the hunger.

"The city's funny," he said. "You think of it as civilized, and maybe some parts of it are nice and safe, but there are brick alleys, deserted buildings, cellars, perfect hiding places for—" He stopped himself, his imagination straining but not quite able to conclude something that had been clear at the beginning. He slipped his arm around her, hoping to offer reassurance, but she only looked at him in an odd way, so he removed his arm, and was glad of it. The wet raincoat had a clinging, yeasty quality. Perhaps she was one of the ugly ones who had come to terms with herself as she was. These were not vulnerable to him, but (his hunger prompted him) this one did not really have that feel.

He pulled the car into a parking space beside many other empty spaces before a building as anonymous as others along this street. The rain washed in rhythmic waves across the roof. He got out and went around to open her door. She would not run and he did not have the strength to compel her. The rain pelted them as they walked from the car to the door of her building.

A flight of stairs carpeted with a threadbare, colorless runner, squeaked, he supposed, familiarly under her weight. The staircase and hallway was dimly lit by flyspecked light fixtures of antique design. The walls displayed their many coats of paint in peeling layers, green, cream, blue, green again. Someone had scrawled obscenities in a childish hand. The hallway was littered, broken toys, bits of mold-colored organic matter. Someone who was not what he was would have felt pity to see the squalor in which she lived, but he was pleased. That would make it easier for him.

She opened the door. The apartment seemed only a continuation of the corridor. Mildew had added subliminal designs to the cheap flower-printed wallpaper. The furniture was that predictable collection of odds and ends that inevitably ends up in a furnished room. There were no pictures, pillows, rugs or books to show that someone had even attempted to make a home here. He was discomfited. That was wrong; they all had the nesting instinct; he depended upon it. Sometimes he promised marriage first and saw the ghosts of suburban ranch houses and magazine-ad children flicker in their eyes.

"I'll put on some dry clothes. I'll bring you a blanket. No, don't turn on the lights. At work my eyes get kind of tired."

He imagined her night after night groping about the darkness like some huge blind grub in its burrow. Why wasn't she being giggly and coy about the changing of clothes? She tossed in a blanket and he undressed and wrapped himself in it.

She came in carrying two jelly glasses with wine in them, her massiveness enhanced by a shapeless bright pink house coat with ruffles at neck and sleeves. It was odd how he was surprised by her bulk each time he saw her. She sat down on the couch, causing him to slide down the slippery cushion until he was pressed against her in the hollow formed by broken springs. Her bloated face swam before him, the image in a bad dream, indistinct in the dimness. There was only the insistence of the rain against the windows. He took her hand or did she take his, and her skin was moist, faintly adhesive. She squirmed out of the robe, her body immense and white, the flesh bulging and folding upon itself. As she put her arms around him, he had the dream-like sensation of warm water lapping gently against his body. At first her largeness was comforting, a great warm wall of flesh, then he felt himself falling . . . into? it? Her body became liquescent and began to engulf him. Darkness surrounded him and when he attempted to scream, his mouth was filled and he gagged. He struggled as the corrosive acids in her body began to digest the outer layers of his skin. As she lolled back she remembered briefly the dark underground place where she had, as one pale larva among dozens, burst from the egg and how she had grown to resemble, through protective mimicry, the occupants of these structures.

By morning her body would eject those indigestible parts, the teeth, the hardest parts of the largest bones, and she would carry them down into the burrow and place them beside the several dozen eggs that she had deposited there. She lay, sated, on the sofa, what looked like a huge woman in a dainty pink house coat. She had assuaged the hunger this way before but she didn't know how many times. It was hard for her to remember. In the morning she might even wonder what had happened to the kind young man who had driven her home.

Valentine

Vern leaned back among the boxes and geometric shadows of boxes, the smeared windows letting in a milky rainy-day light. There was the raw, empty feeling of all moving days and in this bare second-story room, another feeling, one she couldn't quite reach. If she concentrated, she could almost make sense out of the random babble from downstairs:

"Just fill this window with green plants and . . . too big the realtor said, a horror to heat . . . like out of some old Victorian novel . . . cover those cracks with a natural fiber wall hanging. . . . Vern, where'd she go?"

She rose and went downstairs, her footsteps loud against the bare, splintering wood. Just like out of some Victorian novel, she thought, Rebecca descending a staircase. She smiled—long, loose jointed body in faded jeans and work shirt, large hands and feet, a face already a little lined with its intensity, the expression naturally grave—not what one generally thought of as a heroine of romance.

As she entered the kitchen a glass with a cartoon character on it was thrust into her hands. "A toast," said Cash, his auburn hair holding smoldering highlights of dull red even in the dimness. "To Last Ditch House and the starving artists who inhabit it."

Vern sipped the cheap wine, and watched him over the rim. It seemed to her there was a kind of energy about him, never fully used, that was active, throwing off sparks, even when he was standing still. The whole project of the commune had been his and it was still his hand that guided it, though officially all decisions were put to a vote.

By the time cricket-strident darkness had fallen, they had un-
loaded most of their possessions, but a general fatigue had dampened their enthusiasm. The few bulbs they had put into the light
fixtures made islands of light in the darkness. One by one they had
gravitated to what must have been a large parlor. Annie, the weaver,
her face bold and square in a frizz of gold-mesh hair, lay down on
the moldering horsehair sofa, squeezing over and patting a place beside her for Cash. They had made no secret of putting their possessions into the master bedroom. Dennis sat on a footstool, his lanky
height cramped into a posture that threw a vulture shadow onto the
water-stained wall. Dennis was Cash's old friend, but Vern caught
looks that passed between them—something—long burnt out or
a-kindling, not that it was any of her business. Tina sat cross-legged,
a guitar on her lap. Quietly, she began to pluck at the strings. Vern
had never heard her sing, or perform, but only make this distracted,
tentative music. From where she lay on her sleeping bag, Vern could
see the talc-like layer of dust on the floor, disturbed by their comings
and goings, the fine network of spider webs under the sofa. The
house still had a lonely feeling—and that other, what was it? Inde-
finable, a little like anger, but that wasn't it.

They had talked desultorily at first and then had fallen silent.
Vern did not know who had heard it first, but it was certain that it
had been there for some time, growing imperceptibly louder, before
anyone noticed it—a dulled thump, metronomically regular, coming from somewhere above them.

Annie scrambled over Cash and leapt to her feet, her statuesque
form rising in shadow gigantically toward the ceiling. "I can feel
something." Her gray eyes were colorless in the half-dark. Vern
knew she was a party psychic and was probably enjoying being the
center of attention.

"I don't believe this," said Dennis as the noise continued, growing gradually louder, until no one could ignore it.

"It's just some old pipes banging," said Cash, but he sat tensely
on the edge of the sofa.

"Pipes don't bang," said Vern levelly, "unless the water's running."

"Quiet," hissed Annie, putting her hands to her head in fine style. "I'm getting something."

Cash began rummaging in a backpack, pulled out a flashlight. "It's up there."

Vern followed him as he pounded up the stairs, though all the others held their places. The sound was more intense on the second floor, yet still somehow above them. Cash banged about the upstairs, throwing open doors, thrusting his beam of light into musty-smelling darkness. At the back of one room they found a rickety open staircase leading upward. Vern touched Cash's shoulder, the warmth making her realize the coldness of her hand. "It's stopped," she said.

They listened.

The stairs beckoned crookedly upward, but there was silence.

"What would that lead to—an attic?"

"You mean a real attic, with junk in it and everything?"

Cash threw back the trapdoor in a shower of dust and grit. There were trunks and boxes hung with spider webs and cross-hatched with minute mote-laden beams of light from cracks in the roof and walls. The wan circle from Cash's flashlight moved tantalizingly across various objects without stopping to bring them fully out of the gloom. They took a last look around, as Annie's worried voice came to them from the floor below.

When they returned, little was said. Lame jokes about haunted houses were tossed around and the subject was quickly dropped.

Later, in the small upstairs room she had chosen, Vern sat, rolled in her sleeping bag, propped against a wall, a notebook in her lap. For some time she had tried to work on the book of poems for which she had received the grant, but the notebook was filled with miscellaneous jottings and doodles as the time ran out on the grant. She sat there for some moments, looking blank as she arranged the faded designs on the peeling wallpaper into bizarre figures, witches, skeletal trees. In a hypnagogic state she was hardly aware of the tensing of her fingers on the pen, the dry scratch of it across the paper, until she looked down and saw what she had written:

If you and I were one, dear
If you were only mine
My heart I'd give you freely
For to be your valentine.

The handwriting was her own, but the thought that she could write such doggerel, even under autohypnosis, made her a little sick. She closed the notebook and reached up to pull the chain that hung beside the bare bulb, bringing down darkness.

There were no further disturbances for some time, and they settled in, beginning to fill the large, empty rooms with found *objets d'art* and secondhand furniture. Cash had begun in one corner a mural that would eventually sprawl through the whole house. He had chosen as his subject his own interpretation of *The Lord of the Rings*, and it was clear to Vern that in time she would have to lock her door to keep the elves out.

One morning Vern heard bumping noises and emerged from her room, but realized that these were only the mundane sounds of Annie moving a small bureau out of the master bedroom. Without any questions Vern helped her down the hall with it. The rest of Annie's things were in an empty room down the hall, but what she had brought huddled pitifully in a corner of the large echoing space.

"There might be some furniture you could use in the attic. We—uh, Cash and I found it that first night, but somehow I never got back there." They climbed the rickety stairs and came through the trapdoor. Sunlight through cracks and knotholes gilded the trunks and discarded objects in lambent unreality. Breathing the dust-laden air, they began in silence to look through the collection of articles there. Annie held up a dress of fragile cloth with a giggle unsuited to her Amazonian appearance. She unlimbered a rusty contralto: "Ah, sweet mystery of life, at last I've found you." Vern made a disgusted sound as dust rose from a trunk she opened.

"It must have been really funny to have lived back then. You know, so romantic." Vern's attention had been diverted by an old scrapbook full of varied memorabilia—pressed corsages, photographs, yellowed newspaper clippings that had fallen loose and fragmented like leaves on the ground in autumn. The pungent smell of aging paper came to her as she opened the book. "Besides dress sizes here's something else you and she have in common. She was psychic too—a medium."

"Really?" Vern showed the clipping. "Her name was Sarah Kincaid. And by this, her seances were the talk of the neighborhood, table-leg rapping and all that stuff."

Annie read silently, then aloud, ". . . various apports were produced, fresh flowers of a kind never seen in these environs and several black sharp-edged stones." Annie looked puzzled. "What're apports?"

"Mysterious objects produced by the medium, probably from an accomplice's pocket. The medium is supposed to be able to teleport the solid objects from one place to another."

"Don't be such a skeptic," said Annie. "Just because you've never felt psychic vibrations doesn't mean they don't exist." As Vern looked up, for the first time the vague feelings she had been having coalesced into something she would call the presence. Not that it was a person exactly, or that she even necessarily believed in its concrete existence.

In moving out some articles of furniture she wanted, Annie found a square boxlike contrivance with a dusty velours curtain covering one side. "What do you suppose this is?"

"More psychical paraphernalia. Sometimes the medium did her tricks inside this." She rapped sharply on one wall of the cabinet. "The better to fool the suckers—sorry, the believers." She pulled back the curtain and peered inside. In one corner was a heavy iron box with a decorative brass lock. It resisted her efforts to open it, and she assumed it was because of the corrosion that had formed on it. When she emerged into open air, Annie was giving her a needled look, and she realized that it was her perception of the so-called presence that was making her so bitchy. She vowed to shut up about it, but decided to take along the scrapbook of Sarah Kincaid for further study.

That night the thumping began again with a new intensity and a grinding regularity, as if something long sleeping had been newly disturbed. Annie looked at Vern triumphantly, but it was triumph mixed with fear. Cash stood at the foot of the stairs, every line of his powerful body distinct with anger at what he didn't understand. He ran up the stairs, and this time Vern let him go. She decided that in their own individual ways each of them was reacting to the presence. Cash returned a few moments later, looking sheepish, as the noise continued, slamming away at them, the darkness giving it greater distinctness.

Vern could not sleep and leafed idly through the scrapbook. A photograph fell out. There were radiating cracks in it as if it had been crushed, then carefully smoothed. For a moment she was afraid to study the features for fear that it would put a face on the presence. But he was only a man, looking a little self-conscious and foolish, as is the way sometimes with photographs. He had a cropped beard and pale, light-reflecting eyes. She was wondering if he might have been Sarah's lover when there was a knock on her closed door, almost lost in the thumping sound overhead. She pushed the scrapbook under the bed she had recently bought to replace the sleeping bag and went to the door.

Dennis entered, blinking in the light, his eyes a little distorted by the lenses of his glasses. "Come in," she said with a little of the surprise and puzzlement still in it.

"That noise"—he gestured vaguely upward—"keeps me awake. I thought we could talk."

"Sure, take the chair."

He was a writer, too, so that should have given them a lot in common. She wondered if it were possible to build a literary career around "thinking about a novel." She supposed stranger things had happened. At any rate, someone sent him a monthly check, so that his thinking wouldn't be interrupted; but there was one thing about Dennis that could be counted on, his innate gentleness. Unlike, she thought, some overcritical unknown poets one could name, present company included. He was there for some time before she realized that he didn't intend to leave, at least not until morning. She considered sending him away, but was arrested by his vulnerable expression. It wasn't a Victorian novel, after all. She leaned back against the pillows with a lazy half-smile. And this was no fate worse than death.

Dennis stayed only the one night; it was as if he were seeking comfort for some hurt. She only understood when she saw Tina leaving the master bedroom furtively early one morning, like a pale, disheveled ghost. Not that there was any necessity of being secretive; it was just Tina's style.

A thought nudged her. She wondered what the proper Miss Kincaid would have thought about having a commune in her house. Ought to be enough to give her a case of "the vapors."

Foolish, she decided, to think that the present moment could in any way affect the past, or the past the present, for that matter. Each was dead to the other and nothing that happened here now could affect Miss Kincaid in any way or give her one single bad dream.

She paused, wondering about that. She had been having dreams, not really so startling, just fleeting impressions, anxiety. She would be holding something, something shameful, she knew, yet she couldn't force herself to look down on it or even to tell its shape with her fingers. There would be confused voices, shouts, and she would awaken, her heart beating rapidly, the presence very near.

And along with the dreams was the noise, that hollow drumbeat that made the nights a horror. Tina and Dennis had had a violent argument one morning, and by evening Dennis was gone. "I can't blame everyone for being on edge," said Cash as they gathered in the parlor among swimming shadows. With the high ceilings they had never been able to properly light it. "But if anyone else decides to move we'll have to give up Last Ditch House; we won't be able to swing the rent."

"I'm going to move out myself at the end of the week," said Annie, "if those noises don't stop."

Vern looked at her a little accusingly.

"I know, I was always talking about being 'into' the occult, but this is real, and to level, it's scaring the hell out of me." Stolidly, she walked out of the room.

"Damn, what does she want me to do, hire an exorcist? If we split up and stop sharing expenses, I'll have to go back to being a weekend artist."

He shouted an obscenity at the ceiling as the sound began, slowly, mechanically at first, then achieving a steady rhythm. Feeling an unshakable despair, Vern went up to her room. Useless to think of working. She pulled the scrapbook from beneath her bed and leafed through it. She had gone completely through it by now, knowing nothing further of the life of Sarah Kincaid. She looked at the last blank page for some moments before realizing what was wrong. Someone had glued the last page to the back cover, and there was something under it. She tore it open and an envelope fell out. Inside that was a yellowed clipping, an obituary for a Mr. James Whitfield, dead at the age of 32 from heart failure. Vern put that aside puzzledly. The other piece of paper was a letter half burned away. She read the fragment silently:

> Foolish of you to say that you are heartbroken, for I made no promises. I know that time heals all wounds and that someday you, I, and my fiancée, Jennie, will all be the best of friends, but you must forgive me if I leave tomorrow, for I fear that my presence has an unsettling effect upon one of your high-strung disposition. Perhaps we may speak to each other after tonight's seance to resolve our feelings toward one another,
>
> In heartfelt sympathy,
>
> James

When she was putting the objects back into the envelope she saw that it contained one other article, an ornate brass key. Still having only a limited understanding of what had happened, she laid the key on her bedside table and tried to think. That resulted only in a fitful sleep that brought back once more the dream. She awoke in utter darkness with an awful sound in her ears that she first inter-preted as the pounding of her own blood through her veins. It was-n't until she saw Cash's face, like a thumb smudge of whiteness above her, that she realized that she had awakened with a scream. She could still feel the strain of it in her throat. She began wiping her hands on the bedclothes, doubling over as a wave of nausea hit her. The dream had finally brought sure and certain knowledge of what she held in her hands. She recovered after a moment and forced her-self to look down on her hands. "I'm all right." She realized that the sound she had awakened to was the pounding, now seeming loud enough to burst the ribs of the fragile old house. "Get your flash-light. I think I've found the key." She smiled wryly and picked up the literal object from her table. She followed Cash to the attic, ad-miring the play of muscles in his back and shoulders under the thin T-shirt as he climbed the stairs. It occurred to her that she would probably sleep with him eventually if they stayed in the house, but it would only be good clean fun. She marveled at the strength of re-pressed passion that could become something almost alive, a pres-ence that could only bring fear to those who couldn't understand it, to those who could perceive such a love as something alien. As they emerged into the attic, the beam slid glitteringly across dust and cobwebs. Here, in this low-ceilinged place, they seemed to be in the center of that muffled drumbeat, not standing apart and listening to it. There was an awful sense of waiting, pain or pleasure drawn out to intolerable lengths.

"They talked about souls and hearts and matters of the spirit," said Vern, gesturing where she wanted Cash to direct the light. She pushed back the velours, inhaling a strong dust smell. "And we thought it was nonsense, some lack in them, but we never think it might be our own lack, some faculty that time is breeding out of us."

"What?" Her hands closed on the cold metal of the lock, Cash's light streaming blindingly past her. "Nothing. Don't worry, tomor-row we'll all be sane. I guess." The hinges were corroded, but she forced open the lid. In mid beat the sound stopped and a pool of

light gathering at the bottom of the box illuminated a handful of
black, sharp edged stones, some small dried flowers, their petals
fallen away, and a dark, flaking organic mass about the size of a
clenched fist.

Taking Care of Bertie

The place was silent, but it was not a pleasant silence. It was a stifled quiet, a drugged-into-mindless-indifference quiet, the soundlessness of nightmare where patients shuffled down mazelike corridors, somnambulant as zombies, hair matted, wrinkled cotton gowns hanging limp over stumped shoulders. It was an uneasy quiet, broken now by a sudden outcry, a crash of falling crockery.

"Get away from me! You devil, get away!"

A fluster of nurses, doctor's voice ordering a tranquilizer in syllables with the ring of a foreign tongue, sobs, hysterical, diminishing until that circling quiet came round again. In restrained tones, two doctors spoke outside the door.

"Stigmata, self-induced, of course, though I must say I've never seen quite this variation before."

"The world is full of a number of things," quoted the other blithely. "That name she kept repeating. I could hardly make it out. What was it, Birdie, Bertie?"

Behind her the door closed with an authoritative "chunk," and though she'd never been here before, she was at home. She paused, awed for the moment by the small entryway with its terra-cotta tile and darkly oiled wooden paneling. As she walked on into a large living room, dust-powdered indigo drapes filtered the light, leaving the room awash in blue shadow, haunted by the substantial ghosts of sheet-draped furniture. She set down the cracked and peeling plastic suitcase and looked around, a little helplessly, which seemed out of character, even to herself. It seemed she should be shouting for joy, but the high-ceilinged gloom oppressed her for the moment.

How was it, she asked herself, that someone could be so good at figuring things, could see angles where everybody else saw straight lines, could land on her feet, and come down running, if it came to that—how did it follow that someone like Eve Mallory suddenly gets word she's inherited an estate from a rich aunt? This time last week she'd have laughed; that wasn't the kind of thing that really happened. That was the kind of thing that stupid people sat around waiting for while the smart ones picked them clean. She pulled back a sheet and uncovered an immense violet couch, a dust-smell rising around her as she sat down on it. Last week she'd been living in that drafty, roach-infested duplex that Hal had gotten them before his luck and then he, himself, had run out. All the quiet spaciousness around here made her feel uneasy. It might be hard to keep remembering in this place that life was a crap game, with no rules except what you could make up as you went along. Good luck, now; that was almost scary, but she supposed she could learn to live with it.

Though she'd been lolling back on the couch, now she sat upright as a man in a dark suit came in, Cavendish, the lawyer, but she thought he'd make a better undertaker. His white, dry face was set in lines of sad sincerity and his movements were slow and deliberate. He had a way of looking at a person as if he were . . . measuring. She crossed her legs, heedless of the slit skirt she wore. "I didn't know you'd be here already," she said.

"I was making arrangements," he said with a small, sour, smile.

"You do understand the full implications," said Cavendish. "Mrs. Abbott was very fond of Bertie and she wished so strongly that he have good care after her death that she made it a stipulation of the will."

"Sure, I heard all that stuff when the will was read. I still can't quite figure out, though, why she left it all to me. She didn't even know me."

"Mrs. Abbott had become a recluse in the latter part of her life. You were the closest female relative. She chose you as a replacement for herself, so to speak. Here we are." A large-bosomed woman in a cook's uniform was coming in through the door, and on her shoulder she carried a bundle that shrieked and chattered and writhed, trying to be free of her grip. Before the woman had reached them, the thing managed to twist itself loose and, dropping to the floor like a very large, brown-furred spider and dragging a short length of chain from its collar, darted straight for Mallory. Tiny hands caught in the folds of her skirt, and as Cavendish and the cook fussed, the thing climbed, shrieking madly until it was clinging to her neck. An alien face looked into hers, bright, amber eyes, minuscule fangs set among black, rubbery features that reminded her uncomfortably of those of a human being.

She screamed and tried to tear the apparition away from her, but it scratched and clung. Cavendish managed to peel it loose at last, and at the expense of his funereal composure, it hung, panting, against his vest. There was a sodden spot on Mallory's blouse that hadn't been there before, and she was still encompassed in the smell of the beast, an almost rotten smell. She saw that its fur was patchy and graying, here and there the raw pink of an open sore.

"There, there, Bertie old boy," soothed the lawyer. "Really, he wouldn't hurt you. You'll find him very affectionate. He's upset about her death, I expect. Animals are very perceptive."

"Keep hold of it. Don't let it get loose."

The portly lady in the cook's uniform sniffed before speaking. "He seems to have taken a liking to you right away, and that's a lucky thing."

"Mrs. Gibbons has agreed to report to me about whether, or not you're upholding the terms of the will. You must care for Bertie as Mrs. Abbott herself would have."

"You mean I have to baby-sit that monkey, every minute?"

"I thought you understood that." He held out the animal and it reached for her with its dry little hands.

Only the part of her that saw the angles kept her from giving the two of them a few choice words. Bertie nestled against her shoulder breathing out a gust of putrid breath. She could feel its ribcage through the thin fur.

"Mrs. Abbott wanted old Bertie to be happy to the end of his life," said Cavendish.

Mallory managed a smile but knew it looked sick. "All right,"she agreed silently. "I think that can be arranged. I think I can find a way to take care of Bertie."

Mallory lay back among mounded pillows on a large bed with gray silk sheets. The phone was cradled between shoulder and jaw, and with one hand she languidly fed herself chocolates, with the other she flipped the pages of a fashion magazine. The voice on the phone was painfully sincere; it detailed a long and heart-rending series of events. She listened patiently for several minutes, but her fingernails began to tap a nervous rhythm on the slick magazine pages. "Honey, if you could only spare a few thousand, I know I could get back on my feet, and when I felt like a man again, you and I could—"

"Flake off, creep," she said distantly into the mouthpiece and slammed down the receiver. Laughing uncontrollably she flopped back against the pillows. "Poor Hal. What a fool." She couldn't imagine why her so-called former friends thought that her little bit of good luck had turned her into a soft touch. It had been easy to get rid of them; they'd never really cared about her in the first place. It was entertaining, though, to hear the song-and-dance they went through trying to cash in on old friendships.

There were footsteps in the hallway and a gentle tapping, "Miss Mallory?"

"Sure, come in."

The door opened on the white-clad bulk of Mrs. Gibbons, and a brown blur of motion darted across the floor. Bertie crawled across the bed, seepings from his sores dampening the pale silk. Mallory managed one deep breath before the smelly creature embraced her neck, chittering mindlessly next to her ear.

"It seems that Bertie got himself locked into the linen closet," said the cook, her voice edged with suspicion. "I can't think how."

She had been telling herself that the creature was so old it was bound to keel over any day, but whenever it set eyes on her it had to be near her, as it had done that first day, almost as if it understood what its former owner had tried to do. As its bony body writhed against her, she had a sudden, almost overpowering desire to get it by the neck and to squeeze. With an effort the part of her that was good at figuring things out took control and she patted the sparse silvery fur. "Old Bertie is all over the house," she said. "How should I know how he gets into these things. He's clumsy and half blind. Almost anything could happen to him." Mrs. Gibbons sniffed and gave her a direct look, not quite daring to voice any suspicions. The look said that if there were an accident, it had better be plausible.

Thursday was cook's day off, a day with gray skies and a chill in the air. Bertie protested loudly as Mallory tied his chain to a table leg. There were still some servants in the house, but they weren't likely to interfere. She threw some logs into the fireplace. "Perfect day for a fire, Bertie," she said, and then cursed as the match sputtered and went out. It took her some time, but eventually flames jetted from the dry wood. She warmed herself for a moment against the coldness of the large room. She laid the protective screen that was usually in place before the fire over on its back. "Too bad that screen fell, isn't it?" she asked and went over to untie the chain. The monkey climbed happily to her shoulder, but she shivered as she touched that light body, scaly patches of skin showing through the fur, the bones a fragile framework, the breath flavored with the heavy scent of slow decay. She moved closer to the fire, and Bertie basked in the warmth, eyes shining trustingly up at her. Vaguely, she wondered why it was that she loathed the only thing that had ever seemed to feel a genuine attachment for her.

Her hands tightened on the beast's body, and with a gesture whose violence surprised even her, she thrust him into the flames. Sparks caught in the dry fur and there was an awful, an unforgettable shriek of rage and pain and fear, but in the next moment it was as if a part of the fire itself had broken loose and was leaping up at her.

Flames played down long simian arms, framed the almost-human face in a fantastic aura. Fire leaped from fur to cloth as the burning creature gripped her dress. She felt pain as small fangs met in her arm.

She struck at the animal and at the flames, not knowing where one left off and the other began. She thought she felt bones give way beneath her palm as she struck, and she couldn't have said herself what happened, detail by detail, except that when it was over she found herself smothering the last sparks of fire on her clothing and keeping an eye on a small, charred body lying near the hearth wreathed in bluish smoke. Her hands had been burned; she was beginning to feel the first twinges of pain as a wild-eyed maid ran into the room. Mallory knelt by the body. "Oh, poor Bertie," she moaned, one eye on the servant. "I couldn't save you. I tried. I really tried." She wasn't sure what Gibbons and Cavendish would think, but that didn't matter now. She even had burns to prove she'd tried to save the little bastard. Talk about landing on your feet — nobody did it better. And now she was free.

Restraints kept the patient from harming herself as she moved restlessly on the bed. For some time there was only more of the all-consuming silence in the room. It seemed to seep inward through the cold pale walls of the place. Then with a start, the patient regained consciousness. Her eyes inspected the room minutely, as a nurse came to stand over her, uniform a subdued rustling. Her gaze roved, caught at a point in mid-air as if something were suspended overhead. Despite her training, the nurse looked, too, but of course there was nothing.

"No! Get away! Bertie, you're burning me! Your eyes!"

The words attenuated to a shriek, and the patient convulsed against the straps. On the white skin of her throat appeared sudden red marks, the print of tiny teeth, clear until welling blood effaced the outlines. Another nurse joined the first, helping her to give an injection. As the nurse held the patient's arm, another bite mark appeared on the wrist. "Hard to believe," she said in hushed tones, her face shaken a little from its usual professional calm, "that a person's mind could inflict this."

"She seems to see an imaginary demon of some kind. Personally, I'm just as glad it is inside her head."

When this particular seizure had subsided, the nurses left the room hastily; neither would admit that they did so because after these episodes, the air always reeked with the pungent scent of burning hair.

The Skins You Love to Touch

Ginger drove along the winding road, letting her thoughts drift. Beside her in the seat Madge, her mother-in-law, kept up a steady monologue that had to do, Ginger knew, with her views on almost any subject you could name. Ginger thought Madge's views all unutterably stupid, but since she never said so, she and her mother-in-law got on famously. So much so that Winston had sent them out together on this Sunday afternoon on an impromptu antique hunt.

Signs fairly bristled amid the lush foliage of the hillsides; it seemed that every other farmer had stopped cultivating the land to harvest the money of silly, antique-crazy rich women from town. "Only," she thought, reconsidering that idea, "I'm one of those women, too."

She'd always known Winston had money; it was just difficult to connect that with herself, even though she'd been married to him for almost a year.

"Look, look, stop here!" Madge's plump white hand, glittering with several rings, indicated a weathered sign almost hidden in the trees. "Sharkey's," it said in letters rudely burned into the silvered board. Ginger braked the station wagon just in time to make the turn into the almost overgrown drive.

"Are you sure this is an antique shop?"

"In this area it couldn't be a massage parlor," said Madge with an earthy laugh. "Or could it?" Light was cut off by overhanging branches, and the wagon bounced jerkily through iron ruts. There was something diseased-looking about the trees, Ginger thought; probably lack of sunlight. Fat ropy vines twined about trunks that showed patches of phosphorescent white beneath peeling bark. Madge was oblivious to the atmosphere, taking out her compact mirror to study her perfectly made up fiftyish face, the lacquered sweep of auburn-dyed hair.

The buildings were widely scattered in the forest growth—a house that seemed scarcely more than a shack, dilapidated outbuildings leaning to one side or with boards missing . . . a newer, larger structure of corrugated metal seemed to be the shop, if shop it was.

Madge didn't hesitate but pushed open the door.

Inside was an old-fashioned glass display case in which reposed several crude wood carvings, human and animal figures.

"Not much in here," said Ginger, poised nervously near the door. The place unnerved her with its echoing emptiness, cobwebs wagging from walls and ceiling in an unfelt breeze. A harsh chemical smell hung heavy on the air.

There was a clump, scuff, clump from a room beyond this one, and a man emerged from it, walking with a limp. One leg was obviously shorter than the other, making him list to one side, and he held his head at an awkward angle to compensate.

The grin that opened in his almost chinless face showed the jagged snags that were all that was left of his teeth and made Ginger think the name Sharkey was accurate, however he'd come by it. She noticed that his hands, toying with a chisel, were, unlike the rest of him, very clean.

"We were just looking at your, er, wares," said Madge. She had touched the dusty countertop and now wiped her fingertips with a tissue.

"Oh, that there's more like a hobby," he said and went to one side of the room. Dust covers obscured what were obviously chairs by their shapes. Sharkey pulled off one of the covers to display a chair covered in darkish beige leather. The legs and front of the armrests were intricately carved. Ginger had to move closer to see that they were fashioned in the shapes of human faces and hands.

"Ah, the craftsmanship," said Madge.

Ginger didn't like the designs; they were almost too lifelike, and the expressions weren't pleasant. As usual, she said nothing. Madge ran her hand along the top of one armrest and made a small sound of amazement under her breath. "This really is extraordinary work," she said.

"All done here, every bit," said Sharkey. "M'dad taught me to tan the hides and I sort learned the whittlin' on m'own."

"Feel," said Madge, drawing Ginger's hand toward the fine-grained leather. Tentatively, she touched it, then let her fingers run along its length. It had really a strange texture, she thought, velvety smooth and it seemed almost to hold . . . warmth.

"Well, sit down in it. I can see you're intrigued," said Madge. "Can you picture it in your living room, across from the sofa? Divine!"

Ginger eased into the chair. There was no squeak of stiff new leather; smooth warmth slid along the backs of her thighs. The springs gave beneath her and she felt suddenly cradled, although there was something vaguely repellent about the feeling, too.

"I can tell it's so comfortable it's almost obscene," said Madge.

That was the word. Ginger struggled to rise and it was as if the chair clung to her caressingly a moment before releasing her.

"How much?" asked Madge.

"Two thousand," said Sharkey quickly, as if ready for the question as well as for the reaction to his response.

"What, for a chair? That's outrageous!"

"Yes, definitely too much," said Ginger, finding a voice as she rubbed briskly at the places on her arms that the chair had touched. "Let's go."

"But we've only just started to bargain," said Madge.

"Sharkey, telephone." The slatternly woman had appeared in the doorway so quickly she gave an impression of being insubstantial—faded gray house dress, wispy mouse-colored hair.

"If you'll wait right hyer, ladies, we can talk about it some more," he said and went out with the woman, who must be his wife, Ginger thought with a shudder.

"I don't like this place," said Ginger. "Or Sharkey, for that matter."

"He's a little rough. But what a craftsman. I think you can talk him down on his price. I think he was afraid we were going to leave. With these people, bargaining is expected." Ginger looked down and saw with embarrassment that her hands had found the back of the chair and were making subtle caressing movements. Quickly she pulled her hands away, buried them in the pockets of her jacket.

Sharkey had now been gone some time, and Madge paced the length of the room, pausing to peer through the back doorway. Then she went through the open door, into the back room.

"Madge—Mom," she corrected, though she had never said that second word with ease where Madge was concerned. She didn't have to imagine Madge as Winston's mother, though; they had the same steely stares, the same jutting chins. "That man will be back any minute."

There was silence from the back room, and when Ginger could stand the suspense no more, she rushed through the door, almost colliding with her mother-in-law. The room was dim, crowded with cluttered workbenches and low vats in which some vile-smelling liquid sat, topped with clots of greenish scum. Arcane tools lay scattered about, and the tiles of the floor were discolored with dark rustlike stains. Madge was standing as if paralyzed, and then Ginger saw she stared at a workbench on which lay a sheet-draped form.

A recognizably human form. Here and there on the sheet's surface were blotches of red. Madge's mouth was working without bringing forth anything very coherent. The color had washed from her face; the dots of rouge on her cheeks made her look like an aging rag doll.

"Shouldn't we just . . . look," said Ginger, touching the edges of the sheet. "Maybe it's not—"

"No." Madge half-screamed the word. "Can't you see he's taken the skin?" She made a half-stifled retching noise as Ginger dropped the sheet, visions of striated muscle tissue red with blood slipping past her mind's eye.

They both heard the opening of the door, the step, shuffle, step coming nearer; too late to pretend they'd seen nothing.

"Ahhh." Sharkey looked embarrassed, as if he'd been caught with his hand in a cookie jar, instead of this monstrousness. "I wish you ladies hadn't come in here. Now you know my little secret." Ginger hung back, waiting for Madge to burst out with a tirade, but there was silence.

"There's really nuthin' like it, you know," said Sharkey. "Works up so easy, kinda with a life of its own. M'daddy gave me his secret formuler. Wears like iron, too."

"But these are people . . ." began Ginger.

"Only in a manner of speakin'. They swarm in the city like lice—junkies, bums, runaways. My cousin, Mort, he's smart about things like that. It ain't never anybody'd be missed. Nobody cares about 'em, y'know." Madge began to nod dully. Color was working its way back into her face behind the masklike makeup. As they talked, Sharkey had somehow maneuvered them out of the dim workroom. Once out of the place, Ginger felt that it almost didn't exist. They stood in the cavernous showroom where the chair sat in a wedge of sunlight cast through a curtainless window—a piece of furniture, that was all, inert and harmless. Somehow she kept thinking of its smoothness. She felt almost an ache to run her fingers over its surface.

I know the kind of people you mean," said Madge almost meekly.

"It makes the chairs, well, different like, I dunno . . ." said Sharkey.

"Unique," said Ginger, surprised at the firm tone of her own voice.

"Yeah," he agreed, "kinda gives the chair a soul, or that's the way I see it."

"Why, that's very poetic," said Madge, and then she fell silent as Ginger snapped open her purse and withdrew her checkbook.

Sharkey rewrapped the chair in the dust cover and with difficulty carried it out of the shop and loaded it into the back of the station wagon. "Mine," thought Ginger. She couldn't remember feeling this much at ease with herself or who she must become. She owned something that no one else could have at any price.

"You really should try and be a little more careful," she said to Sharkey as she sat in the station wagon, ready to drive away. Now very poised and in control, she could afford to be kind. "You should never leave customers alone like that."

A small gleam ignited in Sharkey's deep-set eyes. "Oh, I always let 'em catch me, ma'am."

"You let them catch you?"

"Sure, it always gets me my askin' price." He cleared his throat and turned his head to spit. "Ever' single time."

Garage Sale

They were driving around the city on a steamy late-summer afternoon, two secretaries beating the heat of their inner-city walkup by cruising through suburbia. Here lawns lay crisp and green under a mist from sprinkler systems, the houses hermetically sealed to hold in the coolness breathed by air conditioners. Stella clacked as she drove, but only because she was addicted to plastic bracelets. She also liked to dye her hair different colors—though mercifully just one color at a time. Jen was to Stella as the wren is to the cardinal, not noticeable beside the more flamboyant display, yet having a quiet style all her own.

"They got it made, huh?" said Stella. "Not having to bust their buns in a dumb office every day. House, hubby, and kids—the American dream, right?"

"I think you made a wrong turn."

"Where?"

"Back there. Some of these residential streets end in a *cul-de-sac*, and—"

"A cool de *what?*"

Jen subsided since it was too late to get Stella going in the right direction. Shadows of low-hanging foliage immersed the car, but only served to intensify the heat. The neat cookie-cutter ranches had given way to older residences in a variety of styles, most of them pretentious, spread more widely apart and set well back from the street.

"Or how about these? Woo-eee!"

As they passed a neo-Victorian horror, rife with gingerbread and flanked about with fountains and marble statues, both of them saw at once the hand-lettered sign poked into the funeral-grass lawn:

GARAGE SALE
TODAY ONLY

"Do you believe that?" giggled Stella, putting on the brakes so suddenly that Jen had to steady herself with a hand on the dash.

"What do you suppose they're selling, the Crown Jewels?" asked Jen.

"As long as it's a bargain," said Stella, her bracelets rattling as she climbed out of the car. The house awed Jen a little as she walked toward it. Stella giggled and pointed as she passed a marble Cupid relieving himself into an ornamental pool .

"I know you love these sales," said Jen, "but every time I go to one, I get talked into buying some worthless junk."

"Never can tell. Today may be your day to find a treasure." Jen looked furtively at the cupolas and the stained glass windows. "A place like this—it could just be some kind of joke." Stella gestured toward a cardboard sign tacked to the porch railing: GARAGE SALE IN BACK, with a scarlet arrow pointing the way.

There was a garage in back, though the builders had evidently not felt called upon to give it the ornateness they'd showered upon the house itself. Though the place was large inside, almost barnlike, they saw to their wonder that it was stacked wall to wall with a jumble of artifacts, furniture of all kinds and periods, clothing of several different eras, tools, household gadgets, and things that defied description.

"I think I just died and went to heaven," said Stella. She began to root contentedly about among the merchandise.

Jen nodded a greeting to the woman who seemed to be in charge of the sale. She sat behind a card table on a tattered chaise lounge of violet brocade, most of her attention claimed by a cheap paperback romance. There was something odd about her, something Jen couldn't quite put her finger on, though certainly she might have been any housewife in faded jeans and a checkered shirt rolled to the elbows, a bandanna covering her head, the fat coils of hair rollers distending it.

"There's something funny about this place," she told Stella, who ignored her, rummaging through a trunk of musty-smelling garments, a moth-eaten feather boa draped about her shoulders. "Something funny," she muttered to herself, and began to move desultorily around the place, seeing an enormous moose head, the bottom half of a store-window mannequin and the photographs of generals Grant and Lee framed in what looked like the seat of a privy.

"What an incredible collection of junk!" she said under her breath. Yet despite her incredulity, she began to be carried away by the sheer volume. What had Stella been saying about finding treasure? She was poking about in a dim corner when she moved aside a Chinese silk screen patterned with tigers. As she did, she drew in her breath and hastily began to apologize. A man sat before her in a threadbare recliner, seemingly staring out at her, though with the reflection on his glasses she couldn't quite be sure. Her apology trailed off as she realized he wasn't moving.

"My God! Stella, he's dead! Stel—" As she turned to run, she collided with someone she at first thought was her friend. It was the woman in charge of the sale; she smiled a small, secretive smile that made her angular, high-cheekboned face seem anything but ordinary, and she gripped Jen's arms to keep her from falling. Jen opened her mouth to scream to Stella, but as she looked, by some trick of vision, her friend seemed small and far away, waltzing dreamily, a gown of blue voile held up before her.

"She can't hear you—not from here," said the woman calmly. Released from her grasp, Jen stood unsteadily before the strangely immobile man in the chair.

"Here? Where's here?"

"A juncture. A pivotal moment outside of time. Do you like him?" The woman removed the man's glasses with a proprietary gesture and cleaned them on the tail of her shirt. Jen saw that he had gentle myopic blue eyes.

"Do I like him?"

"I won't pretend he's like new. The hair's thinning on top, and he could lose a bit down here." She patted the obvious paunch beneath his white shirt. "But in many ways he was a good husband."

"He's your—No, you couldn't be selling—"

"Well, a person gets tired of things sometimes before they're quite worn out. You know how it is." A tiny dark questing head peeped from beneath the bandanna and slowly oozed its length down the woman's face: a snake as big around as a pencil with a minuscule tongue that darted out to taste the woman's cheek. Almost before the image registered, certainly before it was believed, the woman had swept it back under the bandanna with a casual gesture. Up close Jen could see the bulges beneath the cloth move, coiling and sliding.

"I guess so," said Jen, licking her lips and looking back toward the man in the chair. "He looks nice, but—" She hadn't noticed before, but there was a price written in grease pencil on his forehead. $10. "But why does he just sit there like that?"

"Since it's getting late," said the woman, lowering her voice conspiratorially, "and no one else has been interested, I'll let him go for half price."

"Is he dead or—"

"He's fully functional. I'll reanimate him when the time comes."

"Are you telling me you're some kind of . . . witch?"

"That's just a word, but I guess it'll do."

"They used to catch witches and burn them!"

The woman laughed, shaking her head until a darkly patterned tail slipped out onto her forehead and quickly slithered back under cover. "Not real witches, they didn't," she said.

"You must be crazy, and—" Jen looked desperately for Stella, but she was no longer there. A yellow plastic bracelet lay on the floor in a prosaic patch of sunlight.

"Don't expect corroboration from your friend. She was never here. Neither were you, if I don't make the sale."

"What if you do? Make the sale."

The woman smiled. "Yeah, I kind of thought you were interested. Well, you'll have a husband, that's all. Say you met him right after you finished business school."

"That's what I'll think?"

"That's what will have happened," said the woman, looking at her fingernails. They were very long fingernails, polished black, and the tips curved inward.

"Do we have children?"

"For five dollars?"

Jen's fingers moved numbly, opening the catch of her purse. She didn't think she could just leave him there like that, staring into space and sitting in that ratty recliner for all eternity. And then, she hadn't had much luck getting a husband the usual way, so . . .

As she handed over the bill, the woman's eyes caught hers, cool amber eyes, steady-burning as lamps, the pupils a horizontal bar of darkness. Her whisper, grown low and sinister, hung in the air. "Tell you what, I'll even throw in the chair."

"Just look at me, Ben. Sometimes I think you're *glued* in that goddamned chair!"

Ben blinked up at her, his blue eyes so innocent, so vulnerable behind their panes of glass that she felt she could gladly throttle him. It was so predictable, so irritating. Screwing up his face with concentration, he did something to the tv's remote control, and the volume of the football game rose imperceptibly. "Really, Jen, I don't suppose you could come up with this overpowering desire to go out on any night except Monday. A man works hard; he deserves a chance to sit down once in a while." He twitched like a rabbit. "So what's for supper?"

"Oh, God!" A wisp of smoke curled through the kitchen door, and Jen ran to remove the smoking pan from the stove. She turned the water on it, half choking on the smell. Then she stood at the sink looking at the charred and drowned remains.

"If I had it all to do over again," she said quietly, drawing a hand across her face and leaving a black smear. She sighed inaudibly, thinking that no one ever had a chance to do it over, no one. Never.

She busied herself in the kitchen for a few minutes, then returned to the living room, automatically picking up newspapers
from the floor and an empty beer can that had left a ring on the coffee table.

"I burned the chops, so I put in a couple of tv dinners. I figured
you'd like that, you like the damn tv so much anyway." For a moment she thought he hadn't heard her; he sat there immobile, like a
graven idol, blue images from the screen flickering on his glasses.

At last he grunted. "That's just great." he said. "A man works
hard all day and comes home to tv dinners. Some wife I found for
myself."

"Listen," she said, interposing herself between him and the set.
"You're not that big a bargain yourself, mister." For some reason
even she could not fathom, she found that vastly amusing, and repeated it. "No bargain," she said, and laughed until tears came to her
eyes.

Surrogate

Steve was repainting the walls of what had been the guest bed-room when he heard the doorbell. "Diane," he shouted, and certain that he'd done his duty, turned back to rolling a pale yellow swath onto the wall. The new crib, bureau and bassinet that Diane had bought lay under protecting sheets and there were several un-opened boxes bearing a toystore logo. His own attitude was as cha-otic and half-formed as this room. Earlier he'd given up all hope of being a father, and it took a certain effort of will to resurrect that hope. He was trying, mostly for Diane's sake, but turning this room into a nursery still seemed a kind of fantasy.

The bell resounded through the house again, an impatient sound, and he shouted again, this time with less confidence. He put down the roller and listened but heard no footsteps. "Damn, she must have gone out." He wiped his hands and hurried toward the door just as the bell sounded again. Through the screen he saw a young woman very visibly pregnant under a cheap dress whose pink-and-yellow print was very nearly phosphorescent. Her eyelids drooped under a layer of blue eyeshadow, and lipstick more nearly black than red glistened on her lips. Her jaw worked a wad of gum.

"Mr. Winston?"

"Yes, I'm Steven Winston."

He felt a hand on his shoulder and realized that Diane was be-hind him.

"I'm Kelsy Adams," she said, thrusting out a small hand as sev-eral plastic bracelets clacked together on her wrist.

Confusedly he clasped hands with her. "I'm sorry—" he began.

She patted her stomach. "I'm your surrogate mother." He heard Diane's indrawn breath, felt her hand clutch his arm. The moment with its tension lengthened until it threatened to pull reality apart, yet here she was on their doorstep in a splash of sunlight. He'd never seen her before, yet it was his child she carried. Thrown badly off balance, he could feel only anger.

"You had no right to come here," he said. "According to the terms of our agreement—"

"Invite her in," whispered Diane.

"No. No, you'll have to go. This isn't right."

"The neighbors . . . invite her in."

Reluctantly he opened the screen. "All right, we'll talk," he said. "But only for a few minutes." Diane moved newspapers off the divan with a nervous motion. She wore what Steve called her white look—shocked but still functioning. It turned her normal fragile prettiness harsh somehow, masklike, hollow.

"Maybe I should've called," said Kelsy, settling herself on the cushions with the air of a cat getting comfortable."

"How did you find us? The terms of our contract stated that we were to have no contact."

"I got the information from a . . . friend who works in the office."

"Well, I'm calling Doctor Joshua," Steve said. "I think something is very wrong here."

As he moved toward the phone, a dribble of mascara melted down Kelsy's cheek. "I had to go somewhere. I got kicked out of my apartment. Those old biddies said I had . . . bad . . . morals." Diane moved to stand beside her, looking down helplessly. "I didn't know people would think I—" began Kelsy, the rest lost in the tissue that Diane handed her.

Diane made a warning gesture as Steve reached for the phone. "Calling the doctor isn't going to change the fact that she's here. She's not just on paper; she's real."

"But this isn't how it's supposed to be. It can cause terrible complications. It must nullify the agreement."

"I'm causing trouble. I'll go. I'll go and you'll never have to see me again." Kelsy wiped her face, smudging streaks of blackness across her cheek, a strangely vulnerable gesture.

"How can anything be nullified" Diane said. "Look at her. It's your—our baby. What does it matter about your agreements and pieces of paper?"

"I didn't mean to bother you; I just didn't know where else to go, but I see I can't stay here." For all of her protests Kelsy wasn't making any moves to leave the comfort of the cushions.

"Don't go. Not just yet. I'll fix us some coffee, no, some juice, that'd be better." A tentative smile appeared amid the ruined makeup. A simpleminded girl, Steve thought. That was all she was. This agreement might be the only stable relationship in her life. But even as he lectured himself, trying to find some compassion, he was wondering how a simpleminded girl could so easily break the security of a doctor's private files.

After Kelsy had downed her second glass of juice, Diane directed her to the bathroom so she could, as she put it, put on a new face. "I wonder if we shouldn't call the doctor," Steve said. "He shouldn't be so careless with confidential information."

"But what if he cancels the agreement? Did we wait this long for it to be like the other time, when I—" Her voice fell to a murmur. "Lost the baby." Her skin seemed translucent, stretched taut over the fine bones of her face, and he was afraid to say anything as if the sound of his voice would shatter her.

"Here I am, back to normal." The greasy layers of makeup had been replaced, making strangely harsh the youthful contours of her face. "And I'm ready to go. You've been really nice. I'm glad I could meet you even if it was only for a few minutes."

Steve followed her toward the door, amazed that this whole soap-opera episode was to be so easily concluded. "I'm glad I met you, too," said Diane. Kelsy was going out the door, smiling back toward Diane. Steve shouted a warning as he saw her foot in its flimsy high-heeled shoe miss the step. Too late to catch her; he caught Diane, who was screaming and bolting forward. Kelsy had fallen full length on the sidewalk and for the moment she hadn't moved. Diane knelt beside her to cradle her head. "Maybe we ought to get an ambulance," Steve said, but Kelsy was already stirring, trying to rise.

"No, she's all right, but we'd better get her inside." Steve helped her to stand but she didn't seem too steady on her feet, so he picked her up. She seemed small somehow, and lighter than she should have been. He put her on the couch.

Diane was carrying a cheap plastic suitcase. "This was left out by the curb. Her things must be in it."

"But she can't stay here."

"Only for the night. In the morning I'll see that she gets to the doctor's office for a checkup."

"This is crazy." Diane came closer and put her arms around him. "It isn't crazy, is it, for me to want your baby—no matter how it comes about."

Still half-asleep, Steve lurched across the living room on his way to the kitchen to make coffee. On the couch, Kelsy, covered to the neck with a wrinkled sheet, looked like something in a cocoon. Her face devoid of the makeup was youthful. She could be hardly out of her teens, he supposed, and as he looked at her, he speculated on the kind of life that would make a woman agree to the surrogate arrangement. He supposed he should feel pity and responsibility, yet as he stood there he was feeling a kind of anxiety, the feeling that at any moment she would awaken and blink and stare at him with eyes gone ferally red in reflected light. Stupid. He turned away.

As he was drinking the coffee, Diane joined him, her slim elegance enveloped in one of his old blanket-cloth robes. "It's been over a week," he said in a tentative voice. "Don't you think it's time she left to get a place of her own?"

"I hate to think of her being alone."

"But this situation, it's impossible. I can just imagine what the Cartons—or the Pendletons—are thinking."

"I told Midge Pendleton that she's my baby sister," said Diane with a pleased, wicked grin that was uncharacteristic of her.

"But her clothes, her appearance—"

"I've been meaning to take her shopping—get her some nicer things. We can afford it."

"But what about the money, the fee she got for the baby?"

"I'm afraid she has no head for money, poor thing, and, well, who cares about that. It's not as if we ever thought we could buy a child."

He paused. He guessed he had thought so, when the agreement was made. It had all seemed so clear, so businesslike.

"Don't you feel the least bit responsible?"

"Of course I do," he said, "but there's something wrong about this. It's—" He couldn't explain. He could talk about the social and moral viewpoints, but that wouldn't begin to touch it. The wrongness was the kind that made hair bristle at the back of the neck and brought an undefined sound of warning up from the throat.

"What are you trying to pull?" he had burst into the living room, startling Kelsy, who was sitting on the floor putting together a jigsaw puzzle. "I happened to run into Doctor Joshua today," he said, feeling as if he were playing the part of an irate father in a play. Kelsy's condition wasn't nearly so noticeable in the simple cotton smocks that Diane had bought for her, and with the makeup toned down, she looked like a teenager. "He told me that our surrogate mother had missed her last two appointments and that he couldn't locate her at her old address."

"What are you shouting about?" Diane stood in the kitchen doorway.

"I thought the reason for her being here was to care for her health."

As jigsaw pieces scattered, Kelsy scrambled to her feet and hurried to stand beside Diane. He couldn't tell if he were imagining it but her stomach seemed smaller under the loose blouse. It was smaller. Or did it only seem so?

"He doesn't like me," said Kelsy.

"She's afraid of Doctor Joshua," explained Diane, putting an arm around Kelsy's shoulders. "We were going to find another doctor, one with more understanding, but we've been so busy shopping and—"

"We can't have her living here—sleeping on the couch, taking up all your time."

"The couch, I've been meaning to mention it to you. I think it'd be a good idea if we set the guest bed up again in the smaller bedroom."

"But that's the nursery. It's all fixed up."

"Of course it is—it will be. But it's important for Kelsy to be comfortable."

He felt that he stood at a crossroads of sorts, yet how could he be certain that the bulge under Kelsy's smock was really diminished? And if it was, how did one explain it without sprawling over into the kinds of ideas that only crazy people believed in? He only knew that under the murky surface of doing one's duty and living up to one's responsibility to one's fellow man, he hated her, with all the hatred of one species for another.

The nursery was a pale yellow with large decals of teddy bears in various costumes. Huddled in a shadowy corner was the baby furniture. A mobile of glittering plastic animals hung over the bed and Kelsy was reaching up to touch it with a languid motion. As it spun, a music box tinkled out a tinny melody. She sat against the pillow with knees up, the posture easy for her now that her stomach had flattened. The absorption had been a gradual process which Diane had never mentioned, but Steve had watched each change with fascination, feeling a vague sense of loss. The process had given Kelsy an additional layer of fat so that the drawn-up knees were dimpled and her breasts were scarcely noticeable under the pink shift with its print of clowns and balloons. Her face had grown rounder, fuller, and there was never any makeup on it now. She was smiling an odd, secretive smile, thinking, he supposed, that she'd won. He stepped closer to the doorway; a board squeaked; she saw him.

"You scared me," she said with a little pout. He could almost be charmed by it; he could see how Diane might be.

"You scared *me*," he said with a smile that was only an ironic twist of the lips. "What are you, really?"

She looked at him out of large shining brown eyes and was silent. Maybe she didn't know herself. Maybe this usurpation was as natural to her as the cuckoo laying its eggs in another bird's nest.

It seemed equally instinctual when he reached for her, locking his hands around the chubby throat. There was a moment of self-loathing, of unreality before he began to squeeze.

He felt a blow from behind, at first unlocalized until a pain spread through his chest. He fell to the floor, his scrabbling hand confirming the double-looped shape of the handles of Diane's sewing shears. Warm liquid flooded into his nose and mouth and he felt that he was drowning in lukewarm water, but the substance that dribbled out over his hand was red. His fading consciousness supplied a kind of glowing haze to the figures seated on the bed. Diane's expression was both fierce and gentle at once as she looked down on Kelsy's tousled head cradled against her breast. Somewhere in the background the music box was endlessly droning its mechanical lullaby.

Alliances

The tunnel Riska had come through had been dark, heavy with the scent of damp and decay that clung to all these ancient passageways. The room she had just entered was spacious and immaculate, richly arrayed. Lamplight picked pinpoints of gold from intricately woven wall hangings, lingered lovingly on the highlights in hand-rubbed wood. Standing between these two worlds: one of darkness, the other of light, Riska felt a passing sense of unreality. The times she'd spent in this rich chamber were dreamlike at best; one could almost say they'd never happened at all. She emerged fully into the room, letting fall the thick draperies that hid the irregular opening through which she'd come. Once, there had been many openings into the Palace of Ultebre's king, but they had been sealed off. This was the only one left.

Though no one was here, she made herself at home as out of old habit, helping herself to a cup of firebrew from one of several clay vessels in a carven cabinet and settling down in a chair built for someone a good deal larger than herself but made more comfortable with cushions from the bed. She sat this way for a time, lolling back on the cushions as if fully relaxed. Yet there was always an underlying tenseness to her thin body, a hint of watchfulness in the deepest dark eyes.

The opening of the chamber's proper door galvanized some of this tenseness and she sat forward as a man entered, only to lie back again, as she recognized Morrien. His tall, well-muscled body was clad in a short house-robe of linen but the effect was the same as if he wore full battle-armor. Something about him was just naturally imposing, and she didn't think that becoming King had really affected that one way or the other. He carried in his arms a child, plump and vigorous, its bare skin giving off the glow of health.

149

Riska's dark eyes fastened almost hungrily on the child a moment. She felt the weight of full reality returning. If she thought everything that had transpired in this chamber a dream, this child was
proof enough that all had been real. Pink starfish hands groped at
Morrien's face, tangled in his hair, but he only patiently dislodged
the baby's grip and swung her down to the low, fur-covered platform that was his bed and let her crawl as she pleased. "I didn't expect to find your bed so crowded," said Riska, trying for light banter,
and yet finding herself ending with a tone of bitterness. "Do you always share your bedchamber with your bastard children?"

"I supposed you'd be glad to see how well she's growing. Foolish of me, I know, to give you the feelings one would expect of any
woman. I see now that that was only in my imagination that I gave
you such feelings as a gift." The child on the bed had found her way
under the bedclothes and had burrowed under them peeking out
and ducking back again with hearty giggling sounds.

Riska stood looking down at the baby; her face with its high,
angular cheekbones bore a studiedly stoic look. "In the undercity
one buys certain powders to make sure no children are born," she
said tonelessly. "Even magic has its failures I suppose." Morrien
looked uneasy, but then that had come to be his usual look since
he'd become King. She felt his arm encircle her shoulders. "Maybe
it's for the best. I can give her a home here as I promised when you
brought her to me."

The baby had reached the edge of the bed and teetered there,
and Riska who was nearer caught her, and holding her somewhat
awkwardly returned her to the center of the bed. She was silent a
moment. "Her hair *is* very dark." She touched the ragged wing of
hair that swooped against her own cheek.

"But surely this is old business that we've settled amicably between us," she said, turning to Morrien. She put her hand gently on
his shoulder. "I didn't come here to talk of it; in fact I didn't come
here to talk at all." Her arm slid around his neck and she drew herself
closer lifting her face toward his.

She felt herself pushed back almost roughly. "So I'm a convenience here for you, as you make your way in the undercity coming and going as you choose, while I remain a fixed target for any assassin with the will to bring down a king."

Riska's laughter, for all her anger, was genuine. "Are you telling me after the two of us schemed and fought and watched men killed so you could claim your rightful place on the throne you've decided now to decline the honor because you fear plots against your life?"

Morrien lunged toward Riska as if he would do her violence but she dodged away knowing that in a moment her words would sink in. His laughter when it came was explosive, a release for long-held tensions. "I guess in those days I was filled with good intentions and many false illusions as to how a kingdom is held together," he said. "But I don't really cringe at shadows. Just today I've had word of a conspiracy. What's the talk in the undercity about the Cult of Dath?"

"I don't concern myself with such talk. Priests are worse than thieves. They expect you to feel uplifted while they rob you. I know only that the chief priest purports his god to be an ancient one, and that his acolytes swagger about the streets with a certain confidence."

"As I thought. They organize and plot my overthrow."

"I'll find out what I can about them. I can still show loyalty, no matter that you think I lack the finer sentiments of womanhood, but I think I'll go. You've managed to turn me cool with all this talk of responsibilities."

As she turned away, Morrien grasped her about the waist and drew her down beside him on a thick rug before a hearth, its fire banked for the night. "As you grew cool, I began to burn," he said.

"The story of our lives," said Riska, shivering as his lips tickled along her throat. Before he gave her his full attention, she saw him look surreptitiously over at the child on the bed, but the baby had fallen asleep.

Riska brushed back strands of hair on Morrien's forehead as they lay, relaxed but still entangled before the last dying embers of the fire. She decided she'd wait until he awoke before leaving, though that wasn't like her. She had to admit the baby made some sort of difference, even if she wasn't quite sure what it was. Living hand-to-mouth in the undercity as she did it seemed she'd made the best bargain possible for the child. Raised by thieves in the remotest and deepest windings of the labyrinth beneath Ultebre she understood that sometimes these compromises had to be made, but she was beginning to think that this agreement wasn't always going to be an easy one to keep.

Morrien's eyes opened and he sat up staring at her as if she were one of the conspirators he'd been talking about. "I didn't mean for this to happen. I came here to try and find the right moment to tell you. Instead, I—is it you that makes this so difficult?"

"Since you're the one doing all the talking, that seems doubtful. But you're not making much sense. Usually, you don't have so much trouble telling me what's on your mind."

Morrien drew a breath. "I don't know what has been between us these years, if anything at all, but it's ended tonight. I'm to be married."

Riska listened without comment, pulling on her loose-fitting trousers whose cut bespoke the undercity. She shrugged into the shapeless shirt without bothering to fasten it. She went to the cabinet and poured two generous drinks, thrusting one at Morrien. "Married," she said, as if tasting the word, then drank quickly as if to wash away the taste.

"The plans are nearly settled; no one knew of it, but now the news will be released to the populace."

"I suppose she's disgustingly young and beautiful."

"I've never seen her, though I suppose she's young at least. She's the eldest daughter of the House of Hastorran."

"This is no marriage; just an alliance with a neighboring city."

"I don't deny that without your knowledge of the tunnel-ways, I'd still be a houseless rebel, but a King must have a Queen and heir."

"Perhaps, but I don't see what that has to do with us, and what we've had together. It hasn't been all that bad, has it, for all it didn't begin well. Take a Queen if you like, take twenty . . . you'll still wait for my return, as always."

Morrien took her hands gently. "You're a kind of insanity to me. And you must agree that an open doorway into the King's bedchamber is the answer to an assassin's prayer."

She nodded curtly, and your ministers will be sure not to let a thief or worse, through the front gates. She turned away from him to retrieve her sheathed dagger and to fasten it so it would hang hidden under her shirt.

"If you have need of me, your spies know the undercity," she said making for the secret exit, her eyes studiedly avoiding the child, lying incredibly relaxed in sleep on the bed. She pulled the drape aside and a dank scent from the labyrinth beneath insinuated itself into the luxurious room. There was a cloudy bit of liquor at the bottom of her cup and she raised it. "To alliances, no matter how uneasy." She drained off the last of it and tossed aside the cup. The drape swung back, and it was as if she'd never been there, the fire burned away to pale ash, the baby sleeping thumb in mouth.

Riska wasn't certain how many days had gone by, but it was old habit that brought her to the opening into the Palace. She smiled wryly, an oath coming familiarly to her lips, as she saw that the entranceway had been sealed with stones and mortar, a businesslike job. She wondered why she hadn't quite taken Morrien seriously when he talked of marriage and of severing old ties, but this wall seemed solid proof.

If she had thought about it, but of course she hadn't, a secret opening such as this was foolhardy to begin with, in these unsettled times. It was only logic to seal the King's bedchamber off from possible enemies, like the kind of logic that had led her to make arrangements for the child but that still lay like an uneasy weight at the back of her mind. Sitting prominently in a niche in the tunnel wall was a vessel of her favorite firebrew and beside it a newly forged dagger, the hilt chased with silver and set with small winking blue stones. In anger she had half decided to leave the offerings there, but hefting the dagger against her own weapon, she found it superior, and shrugged as she tossed her own worn weapon into the niche. It was true that Morrien would never know his gifts were accepted, but she wanted to leave something here as a token, in case he should change his mind.

With the rediscovery of the network of passages beneath Ultebre, it hadn't been long before the poorer classes and the more unsavory elements turned them to their own purposes, creating a busy city beneath the city. There were many places like the brew-house Riska sat in now where assassin rubbed shoulders with conspirator. She told herself she was there to look over the new blood: mercenaries on their way to sell themselves, or sailors off the ships that sailed *Mir Esquivir.* The latter favored short kilts, making it possible to see something of what one was getting beforehand. She conveniently overlooked the fact that she had been here many times before, and had done nothing more than just look. Still, even that was pleasant enough and she still had some of the firebrew Morrien had given her, which she mixed surreptitiously with the watery stuff served here.

Her attention taken by a kilted sailor who had just entered—Gods, but he had nice legs—she realized that someone had sat down at her table. She looked away and had to look back to reassure herself that he was still there, so unostentatious was he, and so nondescript, the no-color hair, thin, droopy mustache, the gray pajama-garment worn by the poorer classes.

"Shem, that's my name, for the moment," he said under his breath, pulling nervously at his tattered mustache. "Shem, the potter's assistant. Didn't you notice the splashes of dried slip on my clothes? It's important to get such details right."

"Morrien's spy," she said, satisfied as the words made him visibly cringe, though the tumult in the busy place made the words inaudible.

"Let's leave this den," he said, "and walk along Traders Way."

"This is a comfortable spot, and I'd intended to amuse myself awhile," she said with her eyes on the sailor.

Shem only nodded, but began talking in undertones about this one or that one who was a spy or an assassin for the Dath cult, and of agents he knew who had disappeared in the undercity without a trace, until she couldn't look around the place without seeing a prospective enemy.

It was a relief to leave. They walked among teeming throngs through the open air bazaar, and somewhere in the proceedings Shem had gotten possession of the firebrew.

"Excellent stuff," he said, taking a swig, "but then I should have known since it bears the Seal of the Palace. You must have high-placed friends."

"So I did . . . once."

As they walked along, they heard shouts and saw a tall man, conspicuous by his shaven head and priestly garb, at the head of an odd sort of procession. He pulled along a boy of about seven, who screamed and cried, and a woman who pulled futilely at the boy at each step, screeching in thwarted rage. Others in the street drew near at the commotion and in crowd-babble expressed an almost obscene interest.

Riska had often seen the shave-heads with their white robes belted with a girdle of moth-eaten brown fur, eight mangy streamers depending from it. Shem didn't need to say, "A priest of Dath, the many-legged."

"I bought this boy at a fair price," panted the priest, a little overweight and outmatched at least for the moment, by the woman and child.

"Give the boy up to his sacred fate," shouted someone in the crowd.

Taking the firebrew from Shem's hand, Riska took one long pull from it, and then cocked back her arm and threw the bottle, connecting solidly with the naked skull of the priest. He went down in a flurry of robes among the milling onlookers, and she saw the boy break free and grasp his mother's hand.

She saw no more because Shem was hustling her down the

street and turning into a debris-choked alleyway. It was darker here then along Trader's Way which was lit by many lamps, but she could still see well enough to realize that the harmless potter's assistant had disappeared to be replaced with someone cold and shrewd, someone not safe to cross. The chuckle building in her throat over the fate of the priest was suddenly stilled.

"I can't believe that Morrien would entrust this mission to such a blind fool as you seem to be," said Shem. "You risked our anonymity for the sake of a snot-nosed brat. Surely you've lived in the undercity long enough to know that children are a renewable resource."

Riska's palm itched for the hilt of her dagger at his words, though she hardly knew why, since he was speaking only the truth. After a time, she curbed her rage.

"I think the commotion is over," said Shem, peering out into the street. "It's safe to go."

"Go?"

"You need to know more of Dath's cult, and there's no better way than to worship, or pretend to."

A crush of people had gathered outside the entrance to the Temple of Dath, just an offshoot of one of the tunnels, a wide flight of steps built to make the downward progression easier. Riska saw that where the corridor narrowed, shave-pate acolytes were handing out cups of some liquid which the worshipers drank thirstily. An elbow prodded her ribs. "Drink it, but stay by me." The unobtrusive potter's assistant now plodded at her side. With a grimace she swallowed the watery stuff. "Tell me what you're seeing and I'll tell you what's really there," Shem continued.

"I see ornate chandeliers with thousands of candles gleaming in them," she said, stopping to take in the luxury of the place. "And these worshipers, I hadn't noticed before, that they're all noblemen and their ladies dressed in elegant finery."

"Torchlight," said Shem, "and a selection of the poorer folk of the city—a few visiting peasants and their wives, few of them having had a recent bath or change of clothing. Your imagination does you credit. There's also straw on the floor, filthy stuff."

"I see rose colored carpeting with a phoenix design worked in gold."

"There, on the dais, Zostris, himself. They call him Dolatorr, god's man—Dolatorr Zostris."

"Yes! I see him, slender, delicate, like a young god."

"Old, pale and wormlike."

On the shaven pate of the Dolatorr the skin had been scarred open in a spider shape with legs radiating down around his skull. A plate of silver that had been set beneath it winked in the candlelight as the man moved his head. As the subdued crowd of worshipers gathered about the dais, a child was brought in, hair and eyebrows shaven. In the white one-piece garment, the child was sexless, the face angelic with a dreamlike smile.

"Dath brings dreams," said Zostris, gesturing to the crowd, a cluster of rings on his fingers catching the light. The stench of the people there had begun to work its way into Riska's image of them as immaculate gentlefolk. The drug wasn't particularly strong, nor were the images consistent. The floor's color kept sliding from rose to orange. The crowd repeated,

"Dath brings dreams."

"Dath drinks deep," said Zostris. He was an indistinct blur in the flickering torchlight, a pale worm with human eyes. With an expert motion, Zostris cut the wrists, and then the throat of the sacrifice who smiled as he did it. Riska thought how noble it must be to slake the thirst of a god—how handsome Zostris appeared, but the sight was somehow disturbing. She had the sudden desire to fight her way through the crowd and turn Zostris' little knife on him.

As blood poured across the altar, something dark and cumbersome began to climb out of the darkness beneath the dais. Something that had neither the appearance nor the movements of anything human. It crept effortlessly up to the dais, bent over the altar stone to lap at red liquid as fastidiously as any cat. Riska was gripping someone's shoulder, hoping it was Shem's.

"What is that—thing?"

"Remember the drug. It's human, but just barely. In a suit of black fur with false extra limbs—many-legged Dath—he's an idiot Zostris found to play the part. Some say he's Zostris' own son, but I doubt it."

Riska's stranglehold loosened as she began to recognize the human shape beneath the costume.

The ritual went on:

Dath will seduce your Spirits.

Dath will give you dreams,

And drink from you as from a cup.

All praise to Dath.

And the crowd echoed, "Praise!" The weird masquerader slipped away behind a screen and Zostris stood at the edge of the dais, towering over the crowd. Riska expected his head to touch the ceiling.

"Now hear me and do what you will," he shrieked and instantly the crowd exploded in screams and jostling bodies. Shem, who had managed to work himself and Riska onto the edge of the crowd, gave her a brisk shake.

"Come back to the real world. I don't really want to see what it is your heart desires." They picked their way along the wall, the dirty straw in convulsion with squirming bodies. Some people seemed to be strangling each other; others were incited to orgy. With a quick look over her shoulder, Riska saw the child-sacrifice, a discarded doll-shape lying across the altar. She wondered why that had seemed so attractive at the time; it was repellent.

"We've seen what he can do with crowds," said Shem, pulling at his nondescript mustache as they walked the streets of the undercity. "And once indoctrinated they seem to react to Zostris' voice, whether or not they're drunk on his dream-potions. We're certain they plan a coup with distraction caused by wholesale rioting in the streets and an elite army of acolytes being trained somewhere undercity. We don't know their timetable; the strike could be days or years away."

"I don't think anyone of sense wants *that* holding sway in Ultebre. Don't you have a plan?"

"I'm devising one. Morrien said that you know more about the passages than anyone yet living, is that true?"

"I suppose so, but . . ."

"I'll get back to you," he said, and with one last yank on his mustache he strode rapidly away, losing himself in the people thronging the streets.

Riska paced the pavings in front of a fruit vendor's stall on Traders Way. She'd received a message that Shem would meet her here but she was beginning to think he'd done it for the sake of subterfuge alone, because she'd been here an hour and there'd been no sign of him. For some moments there had been a man standing behind her at the vendor's stall, deciding upon what fruits to buy by judiciously pinching them. So intent was he on this business that she almost jumped when he spoke to her.

"The plan is in motion. It's all in your hands now."

"What's all in my hands?" she said, turning to face him, though he made nervous motions for her to stand as she had been.

"As well as being a conspirator, this priest Zostris is a fanatic. He believes that the original shrine of Dath still exists somewhere in the cavernways."

"It's possible; I've seen many remnants of Those-who-came-before in my wanderings through the tunnels."

Shem was nodding. "Good, good, tell him just that."

"I'll be glad to, when I see him, which with any luck at all will be never."

"It will be sooner than that."

Riska's hand again began to itch for the hilt of her weapon. "Tell me my part in this, or—"

"Zostris has already been informed that you have knowledge of the caverns. When his men come to capture you, you must fight only a little, enough to convince them but not enough to get yourself hurt; then afterwards, when you lead Zostris deeply into the passages, it should be an easy thing for you to lose him there. Once the head of the Dath cult is gone, it should be simple enough to disband his followers."

"Is this Morrien's plan?"

"It's mine."

"Call it off."

A gigantic figure lurched from behind the vendor's booth, and when Riska looked for Shem he was gone. It was a moment before she realized she was facing the man who must have played the part of Dath in Zostris' ceremony. He was immense, his shoulders gnarled so that his neck and head thrust out forward, his eyes empty, his mouth lax enough so that spit gathered at one corner and dribbled down his chin. He held huge hands out before him as he lumbered toward her. "Fight just hard enough so they're not suspicious," she muttered under her breath, and was about to turn and run when something tickled across her face. Her fingers caught in the delicate webbing as she reached up, and then the catchnet was drawn tight about her waist, pinning her arms. She saw that a shave-pate priest had crept up behind her. Now she had no choice but to be hauled along the street with the skinhead on one side and Zostris' creature on the other. She wasn't even allowed to curse in protest because every time she let an oath slip, the priest raised a stout ivory staff menacingly.

She was brought into a dim, cool room with whitewashed walls where the catchnet was loosened but not removed. She stretched her cramped arms as much as she could and tested the strength of the net. It was fine but tough enough to have cut into her flesh when she'd tried to struggle. The priest went out, calling back over his shoulder the command, "stay," to the monster that tried to slouch along at his heels. For a moment he stood chastened, head down, then his eyes lit on Riska and he brightened. He lurched toward her, froth forming on his lips as he tried to form a word. Unable to move her arms, she backpedaled until she came up against a wall. Huge hands closed on her shoulders and she brought her knee up as hard as she could.

Zostris was stopped short as he entered by the bellowing cries of his creature as it thrashed about on the floor. Riska saw him at first as a radiant figure, graceful as a dancer, his delicate, pale skin setting off the deepset darkness of his eyes, then she remembered that Shem had something about the drug she'd been given having a residual effect with regard to perception of Zostris, and she fought to see him as he really was. By stages she saw the pale, haggard face, eyes harshly outlined in *kohl* glittering with what seemed a barely suppressed madness. As he approached she saw that his skin was soft as a girl's and thought that he must use bleaches and unguents to make it so. A voluminous white robe enveloped his form, with bony wrists and hands emerging from the wide sleeves to make her think the rest of him was similarly skinny,

"Galk, get up," he said to the creature still whimpering on the floor. It shambled to its feet at the sound of his voice and stood eyeing Riska warily. "If you like her, though one could scarcely think why, maybe she'll be yours later on."

"If that's for my benefit, don't bother," said Riska, "and I suppose it must be, since Galk seems to understand only basic commands and those only as an animal understands them, by gesture and tone of voice. I know what you want from me, my knowledge of the caverns, but this is a poor way to begin negotiations."

"Amusing, you come here by force and you talk of negotiations," said Zostris, "but it's true, you're here because of what you know of the passages." He moved to a small table, draped with velvet as if it were an altar and bearing a silver bell, a few scraps of papery substance and what must have been some relic, a yellowed bone with a bit of brown fur clinging to it. He picked up one of the papery scraps lovingly, and brought it near enough so that she could see that there was some sort of writing on it, characters arranged in lines and a diagram of something that looked like an eight-pointed star covered with more of the alien characters. It looked vaguely familiar to Riska, though she wasn't sure why.

Zostris smiled. "But I forget my manners," he said and lifted the silver bell and rang it. A few moments later an acolyte entered, a child of twelve or so, androgynous with shaven head and in a shapeless garment. He or she carried a tray on which was arranged a series of crystal vials, each containing a different colored liquid and a silver cup. The acolyte smiled sweetly with eyes that were utterly devoid of emotion and stood there holding the tray without moving, an almost sentient table.

"Dath gives dreams," said Zostris, beginning to mix the liquids together in the cup. "But I don't do so badly myself. My sweet little acolytes receive dreams that are enchanting and uplifting, but I'm afraid there's no sweetness in you. Your dreams might be nightmares. Then when I've sufficiently enjoyed the spectacle of you screaming and spitting your rage, helpless at my feet, I may agree to give you release, if you give your will over to Dath, and his purposes."

Galk, having been given the command, moved with alacrity to envelope Riska in his huge arms as Zostris came toward her, bearing the cup.

"I've seen the old books you seek," she said quickly, "and a big altar of carven stone, like an eight pointed star." She was surprised to realize that this wasn't a lie. She'd come across them long ago in her travels through the caverns, and had considered the site only a curiosity among many things lost in time in the passages. Galk was closing a huge hand over her jaw, to open her mouth, so she had to hurry the rest. "It was long ago, so to find it again, a clear memory would be important, but if you want to take the chance of clouding my mind, and have those artifacts lost forever . . ."

Zostris stood for several minutes, holding the potion, then at last he waved Galk away and after a time set the cup back on the tray. "Only because I believe you're telling the truth. I believe you have seen the place. Tell me, what of the books?"

"There were many books," said Riska, glad to see the fanatic light kindle in Zostris' eyes. "Many. The secrets in them, once known, would no doubt make a god of any man. I wouldn't trust anyone when this sort of power is involved."

Zostris returned to the altar to gloat over the fragments, looking around with a paranoid gleam in his eyes. "They'll be mine, and I'll

be able to invoke the god at last, not put on a show for the rabble."
He cursed at Galk and drove him from the room. "We'll leave at
once, in secret."

The dank smells and all-encompassing dark were welcome to
Riska as she led Zostris deeper into the passages. She was at
home here, and it seemed good to get away from the games of
power the surface dwellers played. The catch-net still immobilized
her arms, but she had no fear of Zostris here.

"I weary," said Zostris, seeming to stoop and tighten a sandal
strap. "We've wandered for hours in darkness and all we've found are
caverns filled with vile pagan trash." Zostris had not been enticed by
the caches of rare metals, gemstones and intricately crafted artifacts
left by whoever had occupied these tunnels in earlier times. Riska
leaned against a wall to rest a moment, filaments of webbing cutting
into her skin. She was becoming more certain of the way to the
place she remembered, but hoped that leading him down a few
blind alleys had enhanced his feeling of helplessness, of distance
from all that was familiar.

After a time, she tired of this game, and set out for the place she
remembered. If Zostris were to be lost in the caverns for eternity, he
might as well spend it with his god, she thought with a wicked
chuckle, and no doubt the books and relics would arrest his attention as she slipped out of sight.

"Here, I think this is it," she said, after what seemed like endless
turnings in darkness. Zostris struck a light and lit what must
have been an altar-candle judging from the heavy scent of incense
that rose on the stale air. Zostris pulled her forward toward the block
of carven stone that seemed more impressive than she'd
remembered it. His breath came so quickly he seemed to hiss as he
spoke.

"Yes, this is it."

Light played across a rack that held what must have been hundreds of scrolls of the papery material, and Riska heard him hiss

again as he saw them. "Praise, praise to Dath. He shall reign over men for ten thousand years, and all shall remember Zostris as their deliverer on the seventh of Esrunn."

Riska took note of the date as when the coup was planned; unfortunately for Zostris, he wouldn't be there for the riots. He still held the catchnet loosely, but she sensed he was no longer thinking of her. As he moved the candle, light spilled more widely and showed a cage of some silvery metal, much tarnished and twisted awry by some ancient cave-in, the bars broken where once they'd been embedded in the stone. "What's that?" she asked as her eyes caught a glimpse of something, tried to trace its shape. "Over there, turn the light over there again."

The object in the cage was a dry, organic lump of dust-powdered fur. Something curled-in upon itself, dessicate and dead, perhaps for long ages.

"It's nothing, just some debris," said Zostris. As Riska stood there, her attention taken for a moment by the thing in the cage, she felt a numbing impact that expanded into pain. She reached reflexively for her own hidden weapon as she collapsed on the stones near the shattered cage. She felt a foot turn her over and saw Zostris' white face like a floating mask, a narrow-bladed dagger in one skinny hand. She felt her mouth working, but there was too much pain to form the words telling him that he was a fool, since he needed her to find his way out.

"The secret of the shrine must remain with me," he said, and as if reading her mind, he drew from his robe a bit of organic matter that resembled the dried cap of a mushroom. "You think you're the only one with knowledge, but the priesthood also has its secrets." He closed his hand tightly and waited a few moments to open it again. When he did the pinch of powder on his palm was beginning to glow with dull green phosphorescence. "There is now a trail of light to lead me back to the Temple and to my destiny."

When she turned away from his mocking face, she saw a dark liquid pooling beneath her, running into a little groove cut into the stone. She thought it was a curious thing that the groove led directly into the cage, and she pondered this a moment before she realized that the dark liquid was her own blood.

Her vision had begun to blur, but she saw Zostris busily piling up a number of scrolls to take back with him. After a moment he paused, turned round. "What's that sound? Haven't you stopped breathing yet?" There was a susurration of breathing, loud in the silent chamber; she wasn't sure, but she didn't think it was her own. She saw him stare beyond her, drop the scroll he was holding. Just before he dropped the candle, too, his shriek rattled about the cavern in raucous echoes and she heard the rapid pounding of his feet as he fled.

Hair prickled at the back of her neck, for now it was pitch dark, and she could still hear that regular rasp of breathing, and she was certain it wasn't her own because she had stopped, for the moment. But after a while she'd grown too weak even to lift her head from the cool stone, and she felt herself ebbing away. Death wasn't as bad as she'd thought; there was no struggle in it. After a time it almost seemed she was warmly enfolded, and then the dreams came.

Her eyes opened on darkness and the vague solidity of stone onto which water dripped blackly. Light flickered feebly through the rock-walled chamber from a dancing flame in a lamp of antique design. Her hands were free; she moved them over her head, but she was too weak to do anything else. She saw a clay bowl beside her, half full of something oily, and an odd-shaped container that had been sealed but was now raggedly torn open. She recognized the latter as one of the stored-food containers left by those who'd used the caverns in earlier times. She knew that some of the food in them was still good. A pain, as she moved, reminded her of her wound, but when she reached back to touch it her fingers encountered a sticky, clotted mass. She pulled off a few strands of it, and saw that it was masses of cobweb; an ingenious dressing under the circumstances, but she didn't know who could have come upon her here, this deep in the caverns.

She saw a shape bend to enter the small aperture of this chamber. Even though she knew that she had had her wound tended and that she had been fed, evidently by this . . . thing, its alienness made her cringe away. It was bulky, crouched forward and there seemed to be . . . too many legs. Her cheek was brushed by fingertips that felt metallic in their cold hardness. "Hush, don't look, don't look and it'll be all right." The voice, dry, unaccented could not have originated in a human throat. "There now, don't struggle, I promise—" Two powerful hands were grasping her waist and pulling her against a mass of thick fur. A third hand, smaller, loosened her shirt at the throat, pulled at it, baring her shoulder. The fourth hand cupped her chin, gently steadying her against the mild stinging sensation where her neck and shoulder joined. Just as panic was suffocating her, she escaped again into dreams.

Long years later, when she would try to bring back the content of those dreams, she could not. They were perfectly clear when she was in them, but upon awakening, she was left with strange half-focussed images and colors without names. The dreams were all that saved her sanity. She knew the thing fed her, and she in turn fed it. After awhile she made out its true shape, two short legs for walking, two longer appendages for balance ending in feet that were really large hands, knotted across the knuckles with callous. The third pair of appendages were true arms with smaller, more delicate hands, the palms black and scaled, each finger tipped with a thornlike protuberance. It didn't have the eight legs of the cult's spider-god, but to see it walk-hop about the cavern, she could understand why they might make such a mistake.

It had been emaciated at first, the fur dry and the color of dust, but as it fed, it grew more agile, the fur darkening. Riska learned to accept that she must stay always a little weak so it could survive, but as time passed, she too began to grow stronger.

She had just propped herself against the wall and forced herself to take a few unsteady steps when Dath's strange shape bulked against the light. From two hands dangled the bodies of two large cave-rats. "Now I can hunt," said the being proudly, "and you, as well as I, can grow strong." Riska imagined Dath leaping six-legged after the prey, and it was a funny, rather than frightening thought now. Even the leathery, purple-black face with its glittering black eyes and needle-thin fangs always showing a little no longer held terror for her.

"Soon we'll go above ground where I can find larger prey."

"I can walk now," said Riska. She slipped on a wet stone and could have fallen except that Dath's four arms caught and held her.

"A little longer, you must rest."

"No, I have to get back. There's someone I must warn."

"We too had a mission when we first came, my sister-brothers and I, but the aboriginals captured me. Our group was scattered and I never heard from anyone again. They did me no harm; one of my keepers even taught me your language, but they practiced barbaric rites, killing their own kind to keep me fed, when, as you see, none of that is necessary. Then there was a cataclysm, and they fled, leaving me to starve. Luckily I can estivate when necessary."

"A remnant of the same cult has arisen in the city above; they kill children in your name, and are about to begin a bloody revolution."

"Enough atrocities have been committed on my account," said Dath. "I'll go with you, but not now. Not until you're strong enough."

"All right. I'll rest . . . for now. But I'd sleep better if . . ."

"I've fed full already, but I suppose it'll do no harm."

Furred arms enfolded her and she felt the familiar stinging sensation that she knew would lead to dreams.

Riska felt the same displacement as she always did when moving from the underground ways to the surface. Where she had been, day and night had no meaning, and the night sky, endless and crowded with pinpoints of brightness, gave her a momentary feeling of agoraphobia. Dath stood beside her, gaping around at unfamiliar sights, an ungainly figure in the enveloping cloak that Riska had found. "We're lucky it's night," she thought.

"We're too late!" she said aloud. A swirl of lazy smoke rose from the ruins of a building, and the street was choked with debris, as if defenders had thrown up hasty bulwarks. Here and there in the shadows lay still forms recognizable as human bodies. As Riska watched, a hunched figure moved along the street, pausing at each of these forms, an activity that could only mean the intruder was robbing the dead. She gestured at Dath to move back into the cover of an alleyway, as the figure continued to dart about, moving in her direction. "We must detain him and find out how the battle went," she whispered.

As the despoiler of the dead crept past the alley, Dath leapt out, cloak flying; Riska could only imagine what sort of image registered in the skulker's eyes, but his shriek rebounded deafeningly off the rock walls. A moment later Dath returned, bearing in a three-handed grip, a small, wizened man in ragged dress. When Riska tried to question him, he was incoherent, so she had Dath put him down and back away a few steps. "Has Zostris taken the city?" she asked again, pronouncing each syllable carefully.

"He has," the robber said between gasping breaths, "taken all . . . except that Morrien's forces still hold the Palace. Dath's followers gather at the inner wall; it cannot stand against them till the morning. Please . . ." and here he lay down on the pavement at her feet. "Have mercy on me, Lady Witch—consort of demons. I was only taking what the dead would have no further use for."

She left him there, groveling to no purpose, the words consort of demons making her feel uneasy, The cloak blew back, exposing Dath's awkward shape. In the caverns, dependent on the being, she had learned to overlook how alien Dath was.

They zigzagged across the city, avoiding the places where fighting was still going on, pockets of resistance that could not stand long against the lunatic hordes that Zostris had released. Under a pale dawn sky, veiled with smoke from burning buildings, they saw that the inner wall still held and that Zostris, flanked by Galk and several armored priests, was exhorting his multitudes before the gate from a tall hastily-assembled platform. "There he is, my enemy," said Riska, "the one who commits all this in your name."

"You're still too weak to fight," said Dath. "Let me fight your enemy out of love, though I don't know how we'll reach him, with these crowds impeding our way."

"Throw off your cloak." She heard Dath's rasping otherworldly laughter, and wished that the being had used the word 'gratitude.' Could one love a monster, after all? The crowd melted away before them, giving frenzied screams and trying to crawl over one another to get out of the way of the dark-furred shape that moved with a hopping gait. Riska tried to keep pace, but Dath quickly moved ahead.

Riska watched Zostris; surely he had noticed the perturbation in the crowd caused by Dath's progress, though he seemed not to. Raising long, thin arms above his head, he was chanting the familiar, "Dath brings dreams," which the crowd echoed in full voice.

She saw that Dath had now reached the ladder that led up to the platform, and Zostris still seemed oblivious to anything but the sound of his own voice, the echo of the crowd. Dath climbed more quickly than seemed possible, the crowd ceasing their chant as they saw his dark bulk reach the top of the platform. Galk was still dressed in his moth-eaten spider costume. She saw Zostris lift a delicate hand in a tentative gesture, and begin, "Dath drinks—" and then look quickly from counterfeit god to real and back again. Riska could only imagine what the priest thought in that moment. Faith was one thing, reality quite another.

"Charlatan, I drink *you*," she heard Dath bellow, leaping forward.

From someplace in his robes, Zostris had drawn a dagger. Riska saw it glitter as Dath closed in on him, The sight of the god attacking his own priest made the crowd turn on the shave-skulls in a howling rage. They had been made ready to rend someone; it little mattered who.

From the foot of the platform, Riska saw Dath's clawed hand rake Zostris' face, putting out the fanatic glitter of his eyes. Other priests were diving outward, accepting the mercies of the hostile crowd. Galk gibbered and danced about like an unnerved animal, and before Riska could cry out a warning, he leaped onto Dath's back. For a moment the alien staggered forward under his weight, then a long furred arm reached around to dislodge him, and Dath held his struggling body with the two small hands while battering him with the large ones.

Mewling and blinded, Zostris teetered on the edge of the platform and fell into a pile of burning debris, screaming as he curled and blackened, a maggot in a candle flame. The smell of his burning drove back the crowd.

As Dath dropped Galk's inert body onto the planking, Riska saw more of Morrien's soldiers appearing along the top of the wall. She scrambled halfway up the ladder to shout a warning and Dath leapt lithely off the platform as arrows thunked into the wood behind him, "I thought those were the ones we came to rescue," said Dath in utter innocence.

"Some people lack gratitude," she said wryly.

She saw one she thought to be Morrien atop the wall, but smoke made her vision blur. A knot of men had gathered, babbling and pointing toward Dath. "Let's get out of here, quickly." She neglected to mention cages or worse fates for those as different as the spider-being, but perhaps they were both aware of them.

"You don't want to seek your own kind now that you've completed your mission?" The leathery mask of Dath's face was unreadable, but as in an unconscious gesture, one of the smaller, black-scaled hands was extended, and Riska, now becoming aware of her own exhaustion, reached out to grasp it. Together they fled through the crowd.

Riska awoke and listened to the wind slap at the frail boards of the abandoned dwelling. She lay in a silken, cocoon-like bed suspended halfway between ceiling and floor; Dath had constructed a similar bed and lay sleeping across the room. The alien had grown fatter and lazier, glossier of fur with every day they lived here, Riska thought, but that may only have been that they'd acquired some cattle and there was no further need for hunting. That may have been it, Riska thought, but it was really more than that. The alien was complacent and anxious at the same time, as if awaiting some inevitable event.

Except for the occasional moment of doubt, like now, Riska had to admit that she'd become content here herself, for the most part, though sometimes she longed for the excitement of the undercity, and remembered the times with Morrien. As she lay there, she saw a brown-furred limb thrust from the pale silken threads of the cocoon-bed. Half playful, Riska closed her eyes to slits and breathed deeply. Sometimes Dath would slip furtively to her bed and surprise her with the gift of dreams.

Riska was surprised, although not with dreams, to see the alien cross the room stealthily, looking back for reassurance that she still slept. She continued to lie still, now puzzled, thinking perhaps she should say something. Yet she had the unshakeable impression that Dath had slipped out this way before, into the grainy light of just-before-dawn. Strange, she thought, how days of trust could dissolve in a heart-beat's time, just time enough for a door to open.

Giving the creature a head-start, Riska slid down from the bed and followed Dath's route to a cave-mouth, the opening to the tunnel by which they'd come here. It was camouflaged by dead tree branches, but Dath pushed these aside. The being seemed to have some knowledge of the caverns and soon lifted a round metal trapdoor, sliding down into a hidden chamber.

Riska opened the door a crack and peered inside. There was light, a pale blue luster where no light should have been. She knew she should call out to Dath; re-establish their trust, but there was no way to do so now without Dath realizing how she'd come here. Listening to hear the bulky creature move further away into the tunnels. she hung by her hands a moment over nothingness and dropped. The cold light seeped around a corner, and she went that way, mostly out of curiosity. After a moment she found herself at the entrance to a small chamber.

As her eyes grew accustomed to the diffuse radiance, she saw that a bluish, phosphorescent gel spread across one wall gave off the light. She watched as Dath reached into lustrous belly-fur, seeming to grope deeper and finally to draw out a string of faceted blue-green gems. These were placed with care on the wall where they clung by means of the gel. Riska saw the sparkling thousands already in place and realized they weren't gems at all.

The glitter of the wall distracted her attention, and she didn't manage to dodge out of the doorway fast enough as Dath turned. She knew the spider-being's sight was better in the dark than her own, so it seemed ridiculous to try to hide.

"The mission I once told you of," said the being in a voice made resonant by the close quarters, "was to multiply myself."

"I was wrong to follow you," said Riska. "I wish I hadn't . . ." and in the next breath, "so many; I wouldn't have thought there could be so many."

"I wish you hadn't followed," said Dath. "There are things I owe, but—" The creature was edging toward her with that peculiar grace, now all alien, all menacing.

Riska gripped the hilt of Morrien's gift. "If I thought our kind could share a world, the way we shared—but that's not possible, is it. You're growing an army, here."

The thing shrugged lumpishly, a strangely human gesture that Riska could only think had been learned from her. "We pass ourselves on, that's all. Foolish to worry about what an egg may become before it hatches."

"It's odd," said Riska, as if to fill some idle space of time as Dath crept nearer. "Two years ago had you asked me for this world, I'd have said, 'Take it and welcome.' My kind have done nothing for centuries except to quarrel over and despoil it, and I suppose it's not realistic to think that tomorrow will be different. But, through no fault of my own, I've been made mindful of posterity. The world's no longer mine to throw away." Her eyes swept the chamber; she didn't like the close quarters. She knew that Dath could still move quickly, even though grown corpulent of late.

"Our reasons are the same," said Dath, almost with satisfaction.

"I'll reserve a place for you in my memory."

"Kind of you," said Riska. "But I intend to grow old, remembering you." One of Dath's walking hands came at her like a club as claw-tipped fingers raked across the arm she threw up just in time to save her eyes. The blow threw her hard against the wall, but she kept herself from falling. A numbness immediately began to spread from the scratches, so she knew she'd have to win fast if she was to win at all. Dath must charge blindly.

She tore a strand of eggs from their protecting gel and threw them to the ground. When she brought her foot down, there was a satisfying pop as one of the brittle eggs shattered. Dath shrieked and leapt, so quickly that Riska was almost not ready, but she crouched back against the wall, hoping to make herself a small target. She was overwhelmed for a moment by the smothering bulk, but felt her knife go hilt deep. Warm liquid spurted, matting the fur, soaking Riska's hand and wrist. As the thing recoiled, the weapon was wrenched from Riska's hand. Rather than curling up to die, Dath was wheeling for a second charge. Riska was borne down by the lumbering weight this time, raked by claws, pummeled by huge fists, but she thought that the blows became steadily weaker. Soon they stopped altogether and she heard the rasp of the thing's labored breathing. Desperately, she scrabbled about on the rocky floor until her hand closed on a rough-edged stone. "I think . . . you've won," said Dath in a dry, reedy voice very close to her ear. "But, please, won't you let me bring the dreams to you, one more time?"

Riska felt her grip on the stone loosen a moment, and she found herself actually considering it, such a hold the dreams had upon her.

Since she gave no answer, Dath's face drew closer, the mouth opening upon the delicate needle-teeth. With an effort of will Riska brought the stone smashing up into the being's face, breaking the fangs and making the monster's body convulse with pain. For a moment more, claws shredded her clothing and skin, but the struggles grew slower, and at last she could free herself of the oppressive weight.

Her right arm had gone numb; she had to grasp it with her hand to reaffirm its presence, and the numbness seemed to be spreading as if she had been injected with slow poison. Forcing herself to move, she crept in and out of the chamber, bringing armloads of dry brush. It seemed to take forever for it to catch fire, but when it did, she stripped the eggs from the wall. She fed the flames without guilt, thinking that there was plenty of time for guilt later, if there was to be a later.

When the fire blazed up hotly, smoke beginning to fill the chamber and the tunnels beyond, she rolled the great fur bulk that had been Dath into the flames. The corpse could still contain eggs—hundreds? thousands? And Dath had managed to come back from the dead once, why not again?

She realized she'd almost waited too long to run, hacking and gasping for air as she fled the chamber. The opening to aboveground seemed impossibly far as she leapt for it, once, twice, catching hold on her second leap and by a last surge of effort pulling herself up. She could crawl only a little way from the cave-mouth before being sick and ultimately collapsing.

The rasp of the chisel against crumbling mortar was a loud sound in the silence of the labyrinth, but Riska could feel another large stone coming loose. She eased it from its place and lowered it to the ground, pleased to see a dim light filtering through a heavy drapery on the other side. She couldn't even remember the decision to return here, let alone the path she must have taken, half-poisoned as she had been. She struck the chisel again, the hammer muffled in cloth wrappings still making an awful noise. With miraculous ease the dry mortar broke away, and she removed another stone. Now the opening was large enough to squeeze through.

Before she entered she reached blindly into the niche and her hand closed on the cold hilt of the old dagger she'd left there.

The flickering light in the room came from a low-burning cresset suspended near the bed. It outlined the bulky form of Morrien, lying swathed in fur bedclothes, and beside him, that of his

wife, slim and delicate in a gauzy night-dress, uncovered by his unconscious greediness. The feeble lamplight gave an unreal glitter to
hair that lay in curling wisps about her face, turned the lowered
lashes to frail crescents of gold. Riska leaped to the bed, shadows in
the room giving her lean shape an alien look. No flicker of light
from her knife blade which had gone black with tarnish. The sleeping woman's eyes flew open as Riska sent the blade in hard under
her ribs. Her face contorted. Surely now she would scream and
wake Morrien, but if she screamed, Riska couldn't hear it. She sent
the knife in again and again, till her hands were red to the wrist in
seeping blood. Incredibly, Morrien did not stir. He slept as if
drugged, cocooned in his furs.

As she drew back, her work finished, Riska was startled by a
motion at the foot of the bed. Stiffening, she peered into shadows
and saw the dark-haired child. She was lying with head raised, dark
opaque eyes wide open and watching, giving back reflections, her
fat fists clenched on the bedclothes. Riska drew in her breath, tried
to hide her red-streaked hands, but the small soft mouth of the child
was turning up in a knowing smile.

Rain, sluicing in icy rivulets over her face, plastering the clothes
to her body, woke her at last. She lay in the clearing before the
cave-mouth. As she shuddered into full wakefulness, caught for a
moment between the lingering horror of the dream and a perverse
disillusionment that it was not, after all, real, she decided that she had
been given one last gift, triggered by alien chemicals residual in her
system. She sat up at last, feeling heavy, but glad that the poison was
wearing off. Maybe being alive was the most important, after all,
though alliances formed and dissolved in the smoke of old wars. She
forced herself to her feet and staggered toward the dwelling Dath
and she had shared, wanting protection from the driving rain.

Despite her thoughts of shelter, she stood for some time outside,
gripping the door and thinking of the loneliness she knew she'd find
when it was opened.

www.ingramcontent.com/pod-product-compliance
Lightning Source LLC
Chambersburg PA
CBHW050746250626
47155CB00005B/1940